FUSION

FUSION

21 Stories from the
Complete Creative Writing Course

Edited by
Maggie Hamand

First published in 2015 by

The Complete Creative Writing Course
82 Forest Road, London E8 3BH
www.writingcourses.org.uk

Copyright © 2015 the authors

All Rights Reserved. No part of this publication
may be reproduced in any form or by any means
without the prior written permission of the
authors and the publishers

A catalogue record of this book is available from
the British Library

ISBN 978-0-9576944-7-7

Designed by Jane Havell Associates

Printed and bound in the UK by
TJ International Ltd, Padstow, Cornwall

Contents

Foreword

Our third anthology of writing from The Complete Creative Writing Course spans a variety of genres and styles, and includes extracts from novels as well as complete short stories. All the writers published here have attended at least one of our courses, and some have attended regularly over a long period. During this time they have honed their writing skills, learned new techniques, and received constructive criticism which has helped them develop their work in progress and take their writing forward.

The work in this collection includes coming-of-age stories, historical fiction, crime writing, fantasy and science fiction, as well as stories which handle contemporary themes. I am delighted to be able to present this work to a wider audience.

I would also like to take this opportunity to thank our tutors who have helped the writers develop their confidence and abilities – Howard Cunnell, Christie Watson and Naomi Wood, and to thank Rachel Knightley for her help in the anthology's early stages.

MAGGIE HAMAND
London 2015

Kate Beswick

She Knew She Shouldn't

Rosalie knew she shouldn't do it but if she didn't she would burst. The first time was an accident. She had to pick up her shoes, the only ones that were comfortable, from the little man on Roxbury Drive, and the traffic on Santa Monica Boulevard was terrible. She had taken a short cut down Elveston Avenue and had somehow found herself driving past Dr Lieberman's house. It was late in the afternoon and the sprinklers were on; they made lazy circles of water on the lawn, and the street was so quiet she could hear their whispering noises as they flayed out delicate beads of spray. The soft, private sound gave her a shock, as if she had blundered into an intimacy.

She had been tempted to do it again and again, with the excuse, if she needed one, that she was avoiding the traffic on Santa Monica. Now she had no excuse prepared; the craving was so strong, it was past the need for an excuse. She drove slowly past his house, taking in the details of orange trees, peach trees and palms, past his green Buick neatly parked in the driveway. Sometimes she recognised patients, although she never stopped, of course. There was that director who always wore cowboy boots, and she had seen Donna Reed hurrying out, adjusting her sunglasses. Once she recognised Tony Curtis. You see! she thought, they all have problems.

She didn't mean any harm. Dr Lieberman would know that, if anyone did. She was just interested. Every Tuesday she saw Barbara Rush coming out and once she had seen Jane Withers running up the path. Late, Rosalie thought. She herself was never late. Lateness was symbolic. She was right to be interested because when you see people like Tony Curtis and Van Heflin you learn that everyone has problems. We're all exactly alike. She and Dr Lieberman had worked on this and finally agreed. She just wished she believed it more wholeheartedly. Never mind: Van Heflin. It just goes to show. When she saw him at a party, she nodded and smiled, enjoying their secret bond.

But Gail Fisher! Of all people! She was the one who had told Gail about Dr Lieberman in the first place, and Gail had never said a word. Rosalie was hurt. Hurt and angry. After all, Gail was with Dr Lieberman because of Rosalie and she might have mentioned it. Rosalie didn't expect to be thanked. Well, yes, she did expect to be thanked – at least she expected something to show that Gail was grateful. Then she wondered what else Gail hadn't mentioned, if there were other things about Gail she ought to know. After all, Gail was her friend.

Rosalie felt betrayed, and although she never let on to Gail that she'd seen her – after all, why should she? – the knowledge that someone she thought was her friend hadn't bothered to let her in on such important information drove her past Dr Lieberman's office even more regularly.

Over the weeks, she had recognised several other patients. She liked to park briefly across the street and settle into the silence and the heat for a few minutes, enjoying the mixture of bougainvillea and hibiscus that poured over the white stucco wall next to her car, the scent of honeysuckle from somewhere nearby, the sound of bees in the silence and the sight of the palms and succulents that pierced the sky above the next-door garden. It put her into a dreamy state where just sitting close to him was a secret delight. She didn't stay long; she couldn't stay long anyway, she had a lot to do.

The day she noticed that Dr Lieberman's green Buick was not in his garage, she worried. Was he ill? Had his wife taken him to hospital? An emergency? Maybe he had to make a house call – what kind of emergency would bring out a psychoanalyst? What star had pretended to commit suicide? From inside Dr Lieberman's house, a dog barked. Rosalie hated dogs – they scared her. And dogs didn't like her either, she always felt that. Lying on Dr Lieberman's couch, she had sometimes heard a dog bark from the extension where he lived, but she had never thought it was a real dog. It was just a bark.

There he was! Her heart swelled so hard in her throat she almost forgot to breathe. He was just coming out of his house; not from the side entrance to the office where he saw patients, but out the front door framed in wisteria vines, accompanied by a black dog which stood quietly by his side while he attached its leash. What kind of dog was it? She didn't know much about dogs. It was not particularly big but it wasn't a small dog either. It had quite an elegant pointed nose – very elegant, like an ad in the *New Yorker*.

Her friends the Karps had a dog and it was disgusting how they let it jump in the pool. It could poison the water. She got nervous when Lillian jumped into that pool with the Karps' daughter. Lillian begged for a dog, and Abe enjoyed throwing sticks for the Karps' dog, but Rosalie knew what would happen: she would end up walking the dog herself, trying to make it behave and waiting while it did its business – ugh! She felt it wasn't fair that she would have to do that, plus all the other things you had to do to keep an animal. But now she watched Dr Lieberman with the dog. How nice they looked, the pair of them! Dr Lieberman was wearing a casual polo shirt, a slightly darker brown than the dog's collar. He was quite a large man, handsome, but she noticed he was getting a little bit paunchy. Maybe he should take up exercise. Tennis. She tried to picture Dr Lieberman playing tennis, but the picture didn't look right and she erased it.

'Come on, Mitzi,' Dr Lieberman called. The dog walked a few steps, and paused by a lamp-post. The dog lifted its leg. The whole idea of organising the dog's trip to the lavatory was disgusting – well, it shouldn't be, she thought, watching Dr Lieberman watch the dog – after all it's only human. She laughed.

Dr Lieberman stared into the distance and then fumbled in his pocket for something. What was he looking for? A letter. She rolled the window down and craned her neck, as if she could read the envelope from the car. She was tempted to walk down the road where she could see better, but no one walked in Los Angeles; if she walked he would certainly notice her. She was well parked, at the bottom of this unknown driveway; if Dr Lieberman caught sight of her, he would think she was visiting whoever lived here and he might not recognise the car anyway, he had never actually seen it. She felt sad about that. She thought if they got a dog she would work on her fear with Dr Lieberman and then they could walk their dogs together. What was his wife like? Rosalie knew he was married, she'd heard that somewhere. His wife did something.

Dr Lieberman continued to stroll with the dog. She opened the window so she could lean out and get a better view. He had a very relaxed walk. Confident, calm. A man who enjoyed life. Who understood what life was all about and just – well – lived it, the way you were supposed to. The dog stopped again; Dr Lieberman examined the envelope and when the dog had finished they walked a bit further. Going all the way down Linden, he turned into le Conte and posted his letter in the mailbox at the intersection of the two streets. It was deathly quiet, as if all human life had been drained away and had perhaps concentrated in the UCLA campus two blocks away. The dog stopped a few more times – four times, in fact.

A dark blue Oldsmobile came into sight, slowed down, and stopped. Someone rolled down the window and greeted Dr Lieberman. She could hear their voices, but even in the silence she was too far away to hear what they were saying. The man waved goodbye and drove on – she wondered who he was. Not someone in the business – maybe a colleague at UCLA. She knew Dr Lieberman sometimes lectured at UCLA. Should she go to one of his lectures? The thought made her nervous; what would he think – that she was following him? Maybe she would go with Abe, so Dr Lieberman would understand that she was interested in the subject itself. She would find out what it was and read up on it if she had time.

He had turned into le Conte. She couldn't see him. Without really thinking about it, she got out of her car, and followed, staying on the other side of the road, by the drooping pepper trees.

Le Conte was a less residential street. They walked past Gino's, a small Italian restaurant. She and Abe had tried it out when it first opened but it wasn't as great as everyone said. There were about six tables outside; two couples were having a meal and a man sat by himself, eating lasagne and reading *Variety*. Dr Lieberman didn't pause – the dog pulled him past the restaurant – the food must be pretty terrible, she thought. In her experience dogs would stop to eat anything – indeed, the dog gave an exploratory sniff at the tray the waiter carried, before Dr Lieberman said, 'Come on, Mitzi,' tugged gently at the lead, and moved on down le Conte, into Hilgard.

Rosalie's feet were starting to hurt. How much longer was he going to walk? Didn't he have patients this afternoon? She couldn't go any further, her feet were killing her. She stopped in front of Roger Eden's house, with its magnificent arrangement of hollyhocks, fuchsias and huge kangaroo-paw shrubs.

Dr Lieberman stopped. He patted the dog's head and turned – he was coming back – oh my God – he would see her, standing here in Roger Eden's garden. She didn't even know him! He was Esther's friend. If he saw her he would tell Esther and Esther would think she was crazy. She hobbled on as fast as she could.

There was her car, still parked opposite Dr Lieberman's house in front of the station wagon. She had to get back there before he saw her – quickly! Now! He and the dog weren't stopping. They were on the way home – she didn't dare to run – she would trip – but she did run, in a fast, agonised limp, and managed to get to her car just in time to face the glamorous Janet Hayden, her beauty easily recognisable off-screen despite her uncombed hair and lack of make-up. She was standing in the driveway, glaring.

'What do you think you're doing?' she demanded.

'Oh, I didn't mean to . . . ' Rosalie tried to think of an excuse. Janet Hayden was a star famous for temperament.

'This isn't your driveway,' she said. 'This is my driveway and my property.'

'Oh, I know,' Rosalie assured her. The woman was making a lot of noise and Dr Lieberman was not very far away. 'I just had to stop for a minute.'

'There's a whole road here,' the star said. 'I need to get out. I need to get out now.'

'Yes,' Rosalie said. 'Of course.'

'Now! I could call the police!'

My God, the woman was crazy. Rosalie had heard she was un-balanced – well, she'd been married a lot. She had to be neurotic.

'What were you doing here?'

'Nothing,' Rosalie said. She was terrified of getting in the car and driving – what gear? She fumbled with the key. What now? Where did it go? 'I'm just going,' she said. Was she? She was suddenly in a whirl of nervous confusion – a woman so nervous she had forgotten how to drive.

'I have to be at a fitting,' Janet Hayden cried. 'It's important.'

Dr Lieberman had stopped. A man with a brown boxer had just come round the corner. At the sight of Mitzi, the dog broke away from his owner and bounded towards her. Mitzi jumped up and down, shrieking and baring her teeth. Dr Lieberman pulled at the lead shouting, 'Mitzi! No!'

The boxer growled.

'Hurry up,' the star shouted. 'I have to be at a fitting. Oh, my God, why does everyone do this to me!' Her voice had risen to a shriek. She went on screaming, the dogs growled and barked. The boxer's owner hung on to its collar and shouted, 'Come on, boy! Down!'

Mitzi's hysterical little barks shot through the air as she strained to get away from Dr Lieberman and attack the boxer. Dr Lieberman managed to get hold of her just as a boy on a bicycle rounded the corner. Both dogs barked louder. Startled, the boy lost control of the bike, which tilted to one side too quickly for him to recover and he fell on to the street, the bicycle on top of him. He howled in pain, the dogs barked, Dr Lieberman and his friend both went to the aid of the boy, the star sobbed and Rosalie's panic overwhelmed her. She had just one goal: get out of here! The same panic now pushed her into her car; panic told her to insert the ignition key with shaking hands; panic told her to put the car in gear; panic made her put it into the wrong gear so that the grinding of the gear and the screech of the wheels joined the rising balloon of noise all around her.

Rosalie drove straight ahead, overcome with shame and humiliation. Would the star recognise her again? Probably not – she wasn't important enough. Worse – would Dr Lieberman have recognised her? She drove down Santa Monica Boulevard going nowhere, just away, driving until she had left everything behind and she was just herself, driving, moving forward, driving away until she could forget the scene as if it had never happened.

She wanted to cry but – she couldn't help it – she laughed. 'If I knew someone who did this,' she said aloud, 'I'd say they should see an analyst.'

B. B. Howe
The Peaches

Chapter 1

Plunging the peaches in their innocence in to boiling water had been immensely satisfying. The skins had peeled off perfectly, their baby softness contrasting with the steely hardness of the beautiful hand-crafted Japanese knife.

The handle and blade were perfectly balanced, but, unlike my husband, I was not seduced by the sixty-four layers of Damascus steel which encased its steel core, nor the fact that it came with a lifetime's warranty. But I was mesmerised by the lightning flash of the elegant blade as it sliced through the soft, juicy, yellow flesh of each tender peach.

'She is not coming here!' is what I should have said. My hand came down hard, causing the peach to slip; the slice slithered off the board on to the floor. I bent down to spear the tip of the knife into the offending fruit and flick it across towards the sink. Instead, it flipped backwards, flew towards the door and on to the floor. I stared at it in disgust. I threw the damned knife across the kitchen, its sixty-four layers of steel ringing mockingly.

6 p.m. They would not be back here for another hour. Not wanting to torment myself with the thought of what you could do in an hour, I took one of the chilled bottles of Puligny Montra-

chet from the fridge. Holding it to my cheek I was calmed by its coolness. This was for the canapés, but I needed it now. As the wine took effect I thought of the woman I used to be . . .

Chapter 2

I had driven to the imposing offices of Lloyd Mackenzie; I was early by some twenty minutes. And then I saw him. Or rather the iridescent whiteness of his shirt.

I was wearing sunglasses, so it was difficult to discern what I was looking at. I recalled with a wry smile my illicit teenage activity of surreptitiously 'looking' at men or, rather, at the front of their trousers. Once the object of my curiosity saw me and put his hand in his pocket and vigorously moved it up and down. Men were strange; a genuine mystery. As my knowledge of them grew, I wondered if they were circumcised.

I looked at him, his shirt open at the collar, the creases in the sleeves still present. He must have a tie somewhere, I thought. Speaking on his mobile phone he walked up and down, with the ease of a man comfortable in his body. He was tall, broad, not given to being overweight. But it was his face that was arresting: handsome, square with a hard jawline, tanned, maybe late thirties or early forties, freshly shaved, lips full of generosity and promise. His dark, but greying, hair touched the back of his collar.

One day I would move that collar down and gently kiss the back of his neck, but this was not an idea I could conceive of that morning. My eyes moved down the length of his body, a body I would later claim and write on in lipstick: 'my property'.

His trousers, navy, probably part of a suit. The belt, black leather – I would later learn how soft it felt. There would be a button on those trousers and in my urgency my fingers would fumble, and he would place his hand on mine, gently moving it aside, and with ease allow me access. But for now, I went back to my favourite pastime. In a few months I would know the answer.

I realised he was looking directly at me, crossing the road and walking towards me. I felt hot, my face and ears burned. He smiled and I opened the window, instinctively removing my glasses.

His voice was warm, deep and educated. 'Don't park here – the sign slipped down. I got a ticket yesterday. There is a bay further down.'

'That's very kind of you. Thank you.'

'Delighted to be of assistance.' He strode off, looking at his watch, causing me to look at mine; I had only five minutes left. I parked further down.

In the building I spoke to the receptionist.

'Take a seat. Mr Russell will see you shortly.'

'Eleanor Carter?'

I looked up. I swallowed hard, not knowing where to look, but decorum dictated I look straight ahead at him. I smiled.

'Mark Russell,' he said, his hand proffered. 'Park all right? Damned wardens.'

He showed me into his rooms.

Mr Mark J. Russell, senior member of chambers, very soon my pupil-master, later my lover.

Chapter 3

I was feeling tired. The fine wine no longer appealed. I drank it anyway.

Mark once told me I was the cleverer and more intelligent of the two of us, but he was the luckier one as he commanded the higher salary. But was there a glass ceiling at home?

I took the mascarpone cream cheese from the fridge, filling the peaches. I recalled the first time I met Claudia. She was surprisingly small, a bit on the plump side, probably late twenties or early thirties. Jet-black hair, bobbed, pudding-basin style. Her dull blue eyes, shark-like, giving nothing away, dominated her moon-shaped face. She was over-dressed, or rather under-dressed, her red dress just a little too revealing. She was funny and engaging. I could see why the others might like her.

Mark sat us next to each other, opposite him. It was a dinner extrinsically intended for me to meet his pupil-barrister. I had heard a lot about her and what an asset she was. I just did not realise how much and to whom.

Then I noticed. He was helping himself to food off her plate. Did not ask, just took it. When we left and said goodbye, his hand lingered on the small of her back a second longer than necessary.

The beautiful peaches stuffed with white mascarpone looked vulgar. Like her. Why her? She was no great intellect, rather pedestrian, not beautiful or striking, but perhaps that was it: she was ordinary. And that hurt.

I put the peaches in the fridge. I had enough time to change, then I would make the gremolata for the osso bucco.

Looking at my freshly painted lips in the mirror I recalled the conversation from two weeks ago, when I should have stopped this.

*

I pouted in the mirror. The lipstick was a dark, deep red, almost black. I looked like a vampire. Maybe I should consider botox? I pulled my face taut with my fingers.

'Ellie, can we talk about Saturday week?'

I put the lipstick down and looked at Mark's reflection coming towards me.

'Do you like this colour, Mark?'

'Let's have dinner here, and ask Claudia over.'

I stared at my own reflection, disbelieving the words I knew I'd heard. I felt sick. My throat was dry, my voice trapped. I didn't dare to turn around and face him, knowing if I did I would lose control. Then this would be all about me, my insecurities and my inability to move on. Still staring forward, I tucked my hair behind my ears, a habit I had got into as a child when nervous.

'Seafood and maybe osso bucco – what do you think, Ellie?'

He was still speaking. I swallowed hard, and pulled my hair back to cover my ears to stop me feeling exposed.

'But it's your birthday.' I wanted my courtroom voice but it didn't come. I sounded small and pathetic.

'Yes, it is my birthday.' Mark's voice was mean as he articulated every syllable.

His jaw tightened. The vein in the middle of his forehead pulsed. My husband the pugilist, the Oxford double blue, the 'exceptional legal advocate', the bastard. Why did loving him have to be so hard?

Mark started talking me to as if I was an imbecile, the same slow deliberate manner he used when talking to his criminal clients. It was some small compensation that he was talking to my back, although I could still see his face in the mirror.

'Why here?' I said.

His slate-grey eyes went cold, his pupils contracted. 'I told you before. She's having a tough time, she's on her own, and could do with a bit of support. And I thought this would help normalise things,' he said, using the same measured voice.

'Normalise things – what is that? Oh, of course you screw your pupil-barrister, she makes the mistake of falling in love with you, and then you tell her you're not going to leave your wife. And now you feel responsible, so she can come here, and I have to cook dinner. You will have fulfilled your responsibility and everything will be normal. Is that what it is?'

'You are being a bitch, Ellie. Claudia is having a hard time and yes, I do feel responsible.'

'Mark, do you love me?'

'Why do you always have to be so needy? I am here, aren't I? You, the children, we have all of this,' he answered, with his arms gesturing outwards.

What he really meant was that it was all too expensive to dismantle.

Chapter 4

I was glad I was wearing the lipstick this evening, a talisman, armour. I wore black, more armour, but flattering.

Downstairs I took the lemons and retrieved the discarded knife which was still languishing on the floor. Unlike my husband, I was happy using the same knife for everything. I guessed he took the same approach to knives as he did to women: a different woman for a different purpose. I zested the lemons with unnecessary pressure; cut them in half, forcibly flicking out the pips across the kitchen, juicing the fruit so hard it split in my hand. I cursed as the lemon juice stung.

Lost in my thoughts as I viciously chopped the parsley, I did not hear the front door unlock. I was startled by the bustling noise as the kitchen door pushed open – and there she was: my nemesis. She was wearing a blue-green, sequinned, strapless affair, which made her look like an over-stuffed mackerel. Her bulging breasts threatened to burst out. Trollop. I noted with satisfaction her ankles were fat. I looked at her and felt the desire to slap her hard. But instead I subtly grew at least an inch taller by lifting my rib cage from my hips.

I smiled and said with as much saccharine as I could muster, 'Hello, Claudia, welcome to my home.' Stressing the 'my'. Then I noticed she was carrying chocolates, a gift for the hostess, though she was still hanging on to them.

She opened her mouth and in her Austrian accent said, 'Ellie, you are such a great cooker.'

'It is "Eleanor Carter" to you, and it is "cook", not "cooker", you stupid cow,' I said icily. But of course I just said it to myself, like a thought experiment.

I was still holding the knife; its sixty-four layers of Damascus steel felt very reassuring.

She beamed and leant forward to kiss me. I instinctively moved my head back, and then Mark came bursting through, elbowing the door wider, his arms full of bottles of Pomerol. Smiling, he looked at us both facing each other. She was still holding the chocolates, I was still holding the knife. Although it was pointing away from her, his face changed to alarm.

'Ellie!' He shouted.

'What?' I said, frowning.

'What are you doing with that knife?'

'Nothing, I'm chopping parsley.'

'Put it down, Ellie,' Mark said in the tone he reserved for the slow-witted.

Then I decided with perverse logic that if I put the knife down, I would lose face, and so I was not going to put it down.

'Ellie, give me the knife.' He put down some of the bottles, freeing one hand. The table was full and there was nowhere to put the rest. This was ridiculous. He was treating me like a child and making me look like an idiot.

'Fine. Take it,' I said petulantly. I hated him.

I gave him the knife, handle first. He reached out and, just as he took it from me, slipped, skidded and lost his footing and his grip on the rest of the bottles, which slid from his grasp and smashed on the terracotta tiles. Claudia moved quickly, dropping the chocolates, and tried to grab him. She succeeded only in grasping hold of his jacket as she slipped too. She could not stop him from falling and he took her with him, thudding against the table. The rest of the bottles bounced and scattered. The screeching of shattering glass filled the kitchen. Their bodies, entwined on the floor, were obscene. I kicked away the larger pieces of glass, turning away from them.

The bouquet of the fine rich red wine was tantalising as it seeped into the grouting. The tiny fragments glistened like rubies on the kitchen floor. What a complete waste – I wanted a drink more than anything. I stood transfixed, not sure what to do. Should I get a broom or a mop? I made my way over to the cupboard, trying to avoid stepping on the jagged pieces.

Alarming laboured gurgling, deep guttural sounds, stopped me. I looked over towards them. Then I saw, running away from their bodies, a rivulet, which was becoming wider, and wider, and bright red, very red. And it kept flowing. I realised it was not the wine.

Chapter 5

I stood, paralysed by the sheer horror of what was unfolding. I didn't want to be here, but I had to do something. I dared not move in case something else happened. I said out aloud, 'I am going to call the ambulance,' wanting it to arrive without my doing anything.

'Ellie.' I barely recognised Mark's distraught voice. I did not understand what he was saying. I moved closer to him. He was covered in blood, looking at me in sheer terror.

Claudia looked pale, her lips blue, her pupils dilated. I breathed in the metallic smell of the blood, it was everywhere.

'Ambulance,' he pleaded.

Galvanised, I ran to the phone and dialled 999.

The voice at the other end asked, 'Which service do you require?'

'Ellie, the blood, it won't stop, help, Ellie please.'

I told the voice that there was blood everywhere and it would not stop.

The voice wanted to know what had happened. I said I didn't know but they must come now, hurry.

The voice asked if there was anyone else with me?

Then Mark cried out, his voice hoarse, 'No, please no – '

I dropped the phone, leaving the disembodied voice still asking questions.

Mark, covered in blood, was holding Claudia, but he looked all right. She, however, looked clammy, her body now limp and unconscious.

'Claudie, Claudie,' he whispered as he kissed her face. Then he looked up at me with pure hatred. 'She is pregnant, twins. All she did was love me. You tried to kill her.'

I was confounded. Pregnant?

'Ellie, you were holding the knife. You wanted her dead. I said we would get through this. But that was not enough for you.'

'Mark, you took the knife. You were holding it.'

'I took the knife to stop you hurting her.' He looked down and cradled her body closer to him.

Chapter 6

Only a few minutes passed before I heard the claxon of the sirens.

What I chose to say would change our lives forever. Now I was in control, not the pugilist

Opening the front door, I felt as though I was on a film set. The street was ablaze with blue lights, an array of ambulances and police cars. Ignored, the voice must have decided to send the full panoply of emergency services. It all became a blur, the police talking into their shoulders as they walked up the path, following the paramedics. Uniformed people were everywhere. I directed them through to the kitchen. Somebody said, 'She is in shock.' I realised they meant me.

After frantic attempts to resuscitate her, the paramedics ascertained that nothing could be done for Claudia. A police surgeon arrived and declared Claudia's life extinct. Her body was photographed and the scene made secure to prevent contamination of the evidence. The forensic team took more photographs and aluminium dust was everywhere. Claudia's body was eventually taken to the mortuary to await a post mortem.

Later I would understand from the inquest that Claudia had fallen on to the knife Mark was still holding. He had slipped on the sliver of peach.

*

They said the wound was deep and unforgiving. The extremely fine blade had found the descending aorta, leaving her no chance of survival.

I lost count of how many times I had to say what happened, as the different investigating officers tried to piece together what had taken place. They asked me who Claudia was. I said she was a colleague of my husband. I did not say she was his pregnant mistress. I said very little at first as I was 'in shock'.

Mark and I were taken separately down to the police station. I gave a full and detailed statement and was released. Mark was charged with Claudia's involuntary manslaughter.

Lee Farnsworth
Woman's Hour

I was trying to console Pippa, who had just discovered a large mound of grated cheese that was supposed to be in the lasagne baking in the oven, when Kim walked in, waving her phone in the air.

'That was the BBC.'

'Great,' I said because she seemed happy.

'Great!' said Pippa.

'Yes, it is great! I've got you an interview with Radio 4 in the morning, Simon.'

'How exciting!' said Pippa, clapping like a sea lion.

I was not excited. I did not clap. 'I have a meeting with Gavin in the morning. Can we do it another time? What's it about? I don't even know what it's about?'

'It's about infidelity and it's going out live, so there is no other time to do it. And listen, change your attitude. I worked my tits off to get you this. It's an amazing opportunity and you are lucky that they had a last-minute cancellation. They usually get around three million listeners.' I felt three million muscle fibres contract in unison. 'Imagine if just one per cent of those listeners buy your book, Simon.'

'It's just so exciting,' said Pippa. 'What programme is it?'

'It's . . . it's *Woman's Hour*,' said Kim, throwing Pippa a look.

'*Woman's Hour*! When do you think we should come clean about the fact that I am not actually a woman?' I asked.

'Don't worry, I broke it to them, gently,' she said – gently. 'They need someone who can talk about what science tells us about infidelity and they don't care if you are male or female. They want your perspective, not your allegiance.'

The kitchen fell silent but for the whirr of Pippa's oven.

'You will be great, Simon,' said Kim, stepping towards me and wrapping her arms around the back of my waist. 'I know it seems a bit scary right now, honey, but you will be great.' Still holding me, she turned to Pippa, 'Pippa, I'm really, really sorry, but we are going to have to go. We have got lots to do this evening.'

*

At 9.55 the next morning I was sitting in Kim's office wearing a large black pair of headphones, staring at a grey microphone mounted on what looked like a steel imitation limb. I wanted to be back in the department with Gavin, talking about zebra finches. Kim was sitting beside me. 'You are going to be great,' she said. I nodded.

I felt wired and tired. I spoke to Maddie on the phone when we got back to the flat. 'Remember to smile when you are speaking, they will hear it,' she'd said. Then I rehearsed with Kim until 2 a.m., at which point I could no longer think. I fell asleep before Kim had even made it into our bed but I woke an hour later and stayed awake.

'Just remember what we practised and what Maddie taught you,' said Kim, calmly. 'You will be fine.'

I nodded. This is the last time, I said to myself. This is the very last piece of publicity I ever do.

'Hello. Dr Selwood, can you hear me?' An assured young female voice came through the headphones. I looked at Kim who put on her own.

'Hello, yes, this is Simon Selwood. Yes, yes I can hear you.'

'Great. We are about to begin. When we do, you will hear Hilary introduce the segment. Shortly after that she will address questions to yourself and Mrs Meyer. Please don't ask if we can hear you. Okay?'

'That's fine,' I said. But it wasn't fine. The situation was totally unnatural. My ancestors might have spoken to two or three hundred people in their whole lifetime and I was about to speak to millions. I wasn't adapted for this.

'Good luck,' said the voice.

I took a sip of water and sat waiting, swallowing and thinking up questions that I didn't know the answers to. Kim reached out for my hand. I smiled, best as I could.

'Let's turn now to the topic of infidelity,' said a new voice, warm and soupy. 'It's a topic as old as relationships but we have recently been reminded of its impact by the emergence of allegations about the indiscretions of golfer Tiger Woods. I have been joined on the line by two experts . . . ' – I am not an expert, I never said I was an expert – 'with different perspectives on infidelity. Cathy Meyer is a counsellor who works to help couples to protect their relationships from temptation, and Dr Simon Selwood is a behavioural biologist from Empirical University who has recently written a book that tells us what we can learn about ourselves by studying the sex lives of other creatures. Cathy, Simon, good morning to you both.'

'Good morning,' I said. My voice, muffled by the headphones, sounded thick and alien. I could hear Cathy Meyer's voice more clearly. She sounded older than me. I have never accurately guessed a physical appearance from a voice, but that didn't stop me imagining a small wiry female with curly greying hair.

'Let me turn to you first, Cathy.' I felt myself relax just a little and flicked a glance towards Kim. 'We've been reminded once again of all the pain and anguish that infidelity causes. Why does it still happen? What can we do?'

Cathy Meyer began to speak. She sounded confident. Would I sound confident? 'Well, Hilary, in today's society, couples have less support and are exposed to more temptation than ever before. The number of people we meet and the time we spend away from our loved ones have both multiplied many fold over the last century. It's perhaps inevitable that these things happen. However, I believe that fidelity is a skill which can be learned. In my work I help couples who are committed to each other to learn and, and this is crucial, to practise, those skills.'

Cathy Meyer stopped speaking. I swallowed. I was about to be asked for my opinion. What was my opinion?

'And what does that actually involve, Cathy?' said the Hilary voice. A reprieve. I looked at Kim again. She was miming deep, exaggerated breaths. Apparently I was in labour.

'The crucial first step is to help the couple to develop a shared definition of fidelity,' said Cathy. 'My experience is that every couple has a different definition. It is so important to make sure that both parties share and own that definition. Then we work on practising the behaviours that reinforce their choices and learning to recognise and avoid the behaviours which undermine them. Finally, we establish a framework for regular review.'

I listened carefully. The longer Cathy Meyer spoke the more I prayed that I wouldn't be asked for my opinion about what she was saying. I now had an opinion, but it wasn't a positive opinion. I didn't disapprove exactly. After all, what harm could it do? But I did doubt that the effectiveness of Cathy Meyer's approach had been validated with a large sample of randomly selected couples and matched controls.

'Simon, over to you now. Do you think that the biological forces which compel people to stray are just too strong to fight? Are we simply wasting our time trying to fight them?'

I played back the question in my head. Biological forces? Compelled? Stray? But before I was even aware that I had formulated a response, words began to rush from my mouth.

I heard myself say, 'I'm not familiar with Cathy's approach, but I am sure that there are things which couples can do to protect the sanctity of their relationship.' I liked 'sanctity'. To avoid Kim's eyes I stared intently at the grey, cage-like mesh that formed the head of the microphone as I went on. 'Actually, human beings are among the most monogamous of mammalian species. I don't think we would get so outraged when we hear about infidelity if polygamy was the norm. That said, polygamy does have a small but important part to play in human mating strategy.' That sounded okay. I felt okay. I looked at Kim and she nodded eagerly.

Hilary was speaking again. Why so soon? 'In the high-profile case which we have all heard about it is the male who is the transgressor. Clearly we can't judge on the basis of one couple but, in your opinion, are there significant differences between the genders when it comes to infidelity?'

'Well, the first thing to say is that polygamy has probably been an adaptive trait for both sexes throughout the history of our species. There are more similarities than differences between the sexes in this respect, but polygamy has probably served different purposes for the two sexes. It is almost certainly true that, as a consequence of asymmetries of parental investment . . . ' – I silently cursed myself for using technical language. Maddie would hate that – 'it is likely that in early societies men were less discerning about some aspects of mate choice, because there were fewer implications for them.'

Kim was still nodding.

'Cathy,' said Hilary, 'do you see these differences when you work with couples? Do the men and women you work with have different goals? Realistically, do you think those different biological roles ever be reconciled?' As I waited to hear Cathy Meyer's answer, I glanced over at the small digital timer on the table in front of me. Two minutes and forty seconds had elapsed. There were less than five minutes to go.

'Overwhelmingly, the couples I meet want the same thing,' said Cathy. I thought she sounded a bit irritated. 'If I can just say, I think all of this evolutionary psychology nonsense does nothing but harm.' Yes, she was definitely irritated. 'We are asked to accept that men have a deep primal need for sexual variety. We are supposed to believe that to limit that is somehow to deny the poor things their birthright.' I frowned and looked over at Kim. She frowned back and began to scribble a note on a piece of paper. I watched the letters appear while Cathy Meyer spoke, but I couldn't make out the words that were forming. 'It is nothing but self-interest dressed up in a load of pseudo-scientific rubbish. It's not what I see and I really wish people would stop saying it.'

Where did that come from? I looked back at the microphone and tried to recall what Maddie had said about dealing with aggressive interviewers. Would the same technique work here? And what was the technique? Then I saw Maddie before me, stirring her latte and saying, 'Address the question Simon – not the emotion.'

'Let me put that back to Dr Selwood,' said the Hilary voice. 'Don't men and women basically want the same thing? Is there really any solid scientific basis to the suggestion that men are more inclined to seek sexual variety?'

I heard Kim push the piece of paper towards me across the desk but I didn't have time to look at it. I had to trust myself.

'First, let me say that I think my comments have been misinterpreted. I did not say that men had a primal need for sexual variety.

I am not an evolutionary psychologist but I have never heard an evolutionary psychologist say that either. I actually said that men and women are very similar. That doesn't mean that we are the same. There is a lot of strong scientific data which has shown how we diff– '

'It's not science.' Cathy Meyer's voice hissed. 'It's a lot of conjecture about what happened in hunter-gatherer societies and some speculative theorising about anatomical differences between ourselves and other apes. It's twaddle and mumbo jumbo and frankly – '

Hilary interjected, 'Thank you, Cathy. I do want to get back to the main topic but I need to give an opportunity to Dr Selwood to respond to that. Briefly, please, Simon.'

'The evidence that I was referring to comes from anthropology, contemporary psychology, neuroscience and molecular biology,' I said. In the corner of my eye I could see Kim holding up my book. 'And I do think that we can learn a lot about the evolution of human sexuality by comparison with other animals. That's why I wrote my book.' I was rewarded with a thumb from Kim.

Hilary spoke again in the same even but gently probing tone. 'Cathy, let's put biological differences aside. We now live longer than we ever have, and our society is increasingly fragmented: do you really believe that couples marrying or deciding to cohabit today can learn skills that can keep them together for the next fifty plus years? Isn't that asking too much?'

'I really don't think it is,' said Cathy Meyer. 'That doesn't mean that I think it's easy either. I know that I meet couples every day who want to work at it and I think that means that they have a good chance. I do think that monogamy is under fire and I really wish that people would stop talking all of this pessimistic, deterministic nonsense.'

I looked at Kim and shook my head. Cathy Meyer hadn't

listened to a word that I said.

'Simon, a final word from you. Monogamy is under fire and the scientific community is partly responsible. Do you accept that?'

'I don't accept that at all,' I said. 'That's not what I believe. Science doesn't have a vested interest in perpetuating views about the pros and cons of monogamy. Science seeks to shine a torch – ' I instantly regretted the cliché which would earn me another black mark from Maddie, 'on the truth, whatever that – '

'It's male-dominated science,' said Cathy.

It was the second time that she had interrupted me and this time I felt myself flare. 'Do you seriously believe that men are secretly clubbing together to do research which will help to justify polygamy?'

'Don't be ridiculous,' the voice of Cathy Meyer rasped. 'I'm simply saying that you – don't – have – any – evidence. It's – all – supposition,' she emphasised every word, speaking slowly, patronisingly. Kim told me afterwards that Hilary tried to step in at that point, but I honestly didn't hear her.

'There is lots of evidence,' I said, 'if you would only read it without trying to figure out how you will discredit it before you begin. And besides, it isn't as if evolutionary psychologists are charging couples by the hour to test their unproven ideas.'

'I'm afraid we will have to end it there,' said Hilary. 'My thanks to Cathy Meyer, Director of Love for Life in London, and Dr Simon Selwood from Empirical College.'

There was silence in my headphones. I swung my chair around to face Kim. Her mouth was open. I looked down at the note, lying by my right hand. Stay calm and SMILE! it said in big green letters.

Lucinda Labes
The Branding

'Julie, I'm sorry. I won't go to a branding, especially not a woman's.' I planted myself before the fireplace, where a sulky fire was smoking in the grate.

'But if you don't, the Queen will think you despise her.' Julie crossed her gloved hands over her lap and stared at me with pursed lips.

'How would she even know?' I asked.

'There'll be a whole section of the Place Vendôme set aside for courtiers. We will be shooed in, and counted on our way out; that's how she'll know.'

I frowned at Julie. The flecks in her green irises were glints of amber in the morning sunshine. My older sister by six years, she had shepherded me ever since our mother's death when I was eight. To say I looked up to her was an understatement. Without her, I would still be clacking my rosary beads in my convent cell, cracking the ice in my washbasin every winter's morning. She had delivered me from that purgatory, into the glittering bauble of Marie Antoinette's court, and now she would damn well see to it that I observed the proprieties.

'I'm just so tired!' I yawned.

'What were you up to last night? The theatre?'

'Tric trac, actually. Until three in the morning.'

'Well that was silly, wasn't it?'

I rubbed at my brow with both hands. I wouldn't tell her how much I had lost. She rose, slapped her gloves against my arm. 'Come on, let's go.' She pulled her pocket watch out of her cleavage. 'We have twenty minutes to get there.'

As our carriage pulled out of her street, we lurched straight into a clog of other carriages, all making their way in the same direction.

'Popular,' noted Julie, twirling her parasol.

I felt increasingly sickened at the thought of the spectacle ahead. Once I had seen a man hanging by the neck from the gates of the Bastille. His feet had dangled in the air above me, and I had thought it was a mannequin, an odd remnant from a theatre left on the rails. But then I had seen the hairs protruding above the woollen socks, the worn-down heel on the shoe, and I had felt as though a cold hand was swilling my innards. My legs had become sludgy and heavy, my gorge had risen, and yet I had felt some urge to see the face. And then the sight of his bulging eyeballs, the blue tongue and his swollen face had left me heaving on to the cobbles.

Now I felt the same thickness in my legs, the same sickness to the stomach. We were here to witness the disgrace of Jeanne de la Motte. Impersonating the Queen, she had commissioned – on the Queen's behalf – the creation of a diamond necklace so costly it could have kept the whole nation in boots and bread for a year. This was nothing less than the most expensive piece of jewellery ever made. The necklace had been spirited from the country and the Queen had received the bill. As punishment, Marie Antoinette had expressly ordered the woman to be branded on her left shoulder with a big 'M' for *menteuse*, liar. It could have been worse; at least we weren't going to an execution.

Julie pulled out her pocket watch again, sighed and bashed at the roof with her parasol. The carriage halted and she slid back the grille behind the driver's seat. 'We'll get out here. Pull into that carriage yard.'

'Here?' I squawked.

We were already trundling into a parking space, men stepping forward to grab the horses' bridles.

'Wait, how far is it? Are we going to walk?' I gripped on to my velvet armrests. But Julie had flung open the door. The metallic brightness of early spring sunlight flooded in, making me wince. Cold air blasted up my skirts. Julie's driver was already waiting with a proffered arm. I clambered down, my silk slippers squishing into a steaming pile of straw and manure. 'Ugh!' I yelped. All around us, turkeys bobbed and cackled inside their crates, their wattles swinging red as boils. Clamped to either side of Julie's driver, we made our way out of the courtyard and into the flow of pedestrians heading towards the square.

As the crowds pressed in, I was assailed by the smell: stale body odour, shoes mired in faeces, breath that was a dragon's maw of raw onions, fermented alcohol and rotting teeth. I could never get used to the city's poor, emerging from their garrets in their unwashed clothes. In the countryside, we had grown up just the right side of peasantry, but we had had the forest, its leaf-mould floor scattered with chestnuts, the light verdant and cool. It had been our castle, our canopy. Though poor, we had been sheltered. The city bludgeoned its unfortunates.

I struggled to keep up with Julie. She was marching on, seemingly oblivious to the glances we were receiving from the people around us: men raising their eyebrows, doffing their hats; women staring at us with down-turned mouths. We were dressed in the Queen's new fashion, filmy Grecian tunics, tied at the waist with a silk ribbon, hair unpowdered and hanging around the shoulders. Julie was remarkable in any garment, with her strong jaw, thick lips and green eyes. We must have looked like parakeets in a farm-yard. Tiptoeing through the muck, without so much as a corset or stays, I felt almost naked, as though I'd been stripped to the shift before them all, the hairs on my arms and legs standing on end in the chill air.

As we entered the place itself, we could no longer move. People crushed in on every side. My stomach tightened and I hugged my arms around myself, stepping closer to Julie's driver. Even if Julie was unabashed by our position, it was clear he was alarmed. It was his job to keep us safe.

Then Julie was waving, calling out, and I saw the ring-fenced area in which the other aristocrats stood, raised up off the floor of the place on the wide stone steps of the Opera. Julie muscled her way through, and I lunged after her. Heedless of propriety, I grabbed the first hand that was offered to me. As I was pulled up on to the stairs, I met a pair of pale glittering eyes, a domed fore-head – some kind of cleric, in his starched round collar, but a cleric who had my fingers firmly in his grip. A slow smile spread across his delicate face. I noted the thick blond hair, beautifully powdered in the old style.

'I didn't expect to find a Grecian goddess in this crowd,' he murmured, and he applied subtle pressure to my fingertips.

I pulled my hand away and stammered out my name. 'Adelaide de Filleul Billarderie.' I don't know why I gave my maiden name.

'I know who you are,' he said. 'Are you not the Comtesse de Flahaut?'

I nodded and brought a hand to my chest, which was reddening beneath his gaze. Before I had time to ask his name, the crowd sent out a roar and I turned. I gasped. Beneath me, the crowd stretched out, at least two thousand thick. In its midst was a platform, on which two giant men in black held a woman, naked from the waist up, one arm held aloft by each man. The woman threw herself violently from side to side, trying with all her strength to escape the men's grip. As she thrashed, her large pale bosoms swung. I shuddered. To have one's breasts bared in public was surely punishment enough, whatever this woman had done to the Queen. Yet there, on the platform, was the branding sconce, its flame twisting in the wind.

'Nuts?' Another man, an old friend of my sister's, had pressed forward to stand by us, and was holding out a paper bag of caramelised almonds. I reeled back, appalled. Surely this was not an occasion that warranted snacks?

My sister plunged her hand into the bag, crunching at the nuts as she scanned the group of aristocrats for other friends. She waved and smiled at some ladies at the back, her gloved fingers crumbed with toffee. I heaved in a breath, trying to dispel my nausea. I could feel the cleric watching me.

'Lost your appetite?'

I nodded.

'Is this your first time?'

'Yes. You?'

'I've seen executions. Only a couple. Not really my thing. But sometimes one is obliged.' He shrugged, rejected the nuts, then nodded in the direction of the stage. 'This one got off lightly.'

A small man in sombre clothes stepped forward towards the crowd. In one hand he held the branding iron, in the other a large sheet of paper. He shook the iron at the crowd, held up the paper and began to read:

'Jeanne de Valois Saint-Remy, Comtesse de la Motte, you have impugned the dignity of our most revered and holy Queen, Marie Antoinette of France.'

At her name, there was an explosion of noise, some in the

crowd shouting 'Vive la Reine,' but many others jeering and cursing. I was astonished. I knew the Queen's star was low, but for people to openly defame her seemed a new and terrible precedent.

'You have imitated the Queen's sacred person. You have imitated her, and then imitated her in low and disgraceful conduct.' At this there was loud laughter from the crowd. The speaker paused and then forged forward. 'Worse, you have ordered goods on the Queen's behalf.'

'Goods! More goods for a greedy spendthrift!' shouted someone in the crowd. 'Harlot!' shouted another voice. There was a roar, and a group of royal guardsmen began surging through the people, silencing the hecklers immediately.

The speaker continued. 'For this, you will be forever branded with an "M" for *menteuse*.' And with that he plunged the branding iron into the flame. The crowd stilled, as though holding its breath. The seconds passed. The big black 'M' on the end of the stick began to glow, dimly then brighter and brighter, until its violent orange colour could be seen across the whole marketplace. The woman was screaming now, her eyes rolling, straining away from the implement.

I could barely breathe. Would no one stop this? I brought my hands to my face, covered my nose and mouth. I felt a low pulse in my groin, a primal dread. Beside me, the cleric was watching, still as a snake before the strike.

The men in black wrenched Jeanne de la Motte forward. She wailed, hunching her shoulders together so that her chest caved away from the brand. The men jerked her back by the arm sockets, exposing her chest and, at the same moment, the spokesman jabbed the iron at her shoulder. She reared back. The power of her fear knocked one arm clean from the grip of one of the huge men, and the brand, instead of hitting her shoulder as instructed, brushed the underside of her breast. Panicked, the brander pushed it into her skin anyway, and the woman gave an unearthly scream as the skin sizzled. My hands flew to my mouth. My eyes smarted with tears. Only a woman could imagine the pain.

The brander pulled away, and La Motte's screams shattered the air, a throbbing red 'M' swelling on the milky underside of her breast. The Queen's lesson had been imprinted on a woman's flesh. We were to know, if we hadn't before, that her reputation was not to be trifled with.

The whole crowd seemed subdued, shamefaced. Just by being here, we were all complicit. People began to drift away, heads bowed, back to their work.

'You are trembling,' said the man. He was staring at me quizzically, as if surprised at my horror.

'That was terrible,' I whispered, shaking my head.

'I will walk you back to your carriage,' he said.

We began to make our way down the steps to the paving below, and it was only then that I realised that the man walked with a stick, his left foot dragging along beside him in an iron box. Inside the box, his foot was encased in an immaculate white stocking, but there was something odd about the shape, as though the bones had been removed, leaving just a flattened pulp of silk-muffled flesh. I averted my gaze. Julie's driver was clearing our way ahead.

The streets were coming back to life around us. A metal works clanged into action, as though a thousand pots were being hammered at once. Carts barged past, piled with mud-caked greens and grizzled cabbages. I could still hear the woman's scream in my ears. When we reached the carriage, the cleric bowed at us as we were helped in. I could feel his stare boring into my behind as I clambered up.

'Who was that?' I gasped as the carriage moved away.

'Charles Maurice de Talleyrand Perigord, one of the most unscrupulous men in all Paris,' said Julie. And then she cocked an eyebrow at me. 'I should have introduced you.' She winked. 'He'll go far.'

Carina Swantee
Sunsets Over the Bay

In the smallest bedroom in the cottage, Walt had painted a sunset straight on to the wall. On the other wall, he'd painted an abstract motif that took up half the space, with thick layers of oil paint, which took years to dry. Sometimes on those endless summer days Celia would put a finger on to it and then slightly, gently, poke into the thick paint and her fingertip would sink in, move the paint, wrinkle it just a little bit. Around that painting Walt mounted a dark red frame, which he nailed straight on to the wall.

It was not that Walt wasn't a painter; he was, by all means. And he loved the idea of being one. The problem was that he wasn't very good at it. Yet. Maybe it was because he didn't get any further; despite his passion and eagerness, he had got stuck with mainly one motif, which was the sunset over the bay. Over and over again, from different angles and distances, he painted the sky and the water in burning colours, dramatic stripes of blue, red and yellow. Then he painted the smooth cliffs and a dark stand of trees surrounding the bay. Sometimes he painted on a canvas, but more often he would take anything else, a piece of plywood or any wood that had once served some purpose in the cottage. Or he would paint the old furniture in the house, striking strands of colours on old chairs or chests, or maybe an orange flower in each corner, and why not some flying black birds on the back? Most of all, he would never leave anything unsigned:

Walt.

There was something intimidating about that room. When Walt was forever gone, Joshua hung wallpaper with little white roses on the walls; assisted by Leah, his young and pregnant wife, who carefully stroked even layers of glue on the back of the rolls and moved around slowly in the room, dressed in huge overalls.

When Celia would come on one of her scarce summer visits, she liked sleeping in that room, knowing that, below the stained and worn-out wallpaper, the old wild paintings were lingering. Although Joshua claimed that he had painted a few layers of white over them, so that the colours would not glow through the wall-paper.

*

'So, what shall we do with all the paintings?' Celia asked after she had finally gathered enough energy to phone her brother. She stood by the side table, next to the wall with the invisible oil painting. Her hair was tucked in under a scarf and she was coated with dust after spending the entire day on the attic.

The old handset was cold and heavy. Celia was only used to talking on her mobile, and she took great care to speak in to the round red receiver which, with its small holes, reminded her of a colander, in to which the words were dropped before they followed the telephone line all the way into town. She imagined the inside full of dried-up saliva, a sort of limescale made of voices derived from ancient upset conversations.

'Oh, Christ! Do we have to go through that now?' Joshua said, irritated. 'I don't know. I don't want them!'

Celia waited, running the curly cord between her fingers.

'I mean, I could take a few,' he added, with a touch of guilt in his voice. 'And I'll ask Mandy. And Alex as well.'

'We could ask Lillian, if she wants one or two, and maybe even for Jenny and Frankie. And why not their kids as well? I mean, for when they get older?' Celia suddenly felt hopeful. Maybe they could spread the paintings out among them. They had grown in to a considerable group, their children had grown up and even Lillian was a grandmother now. 'It's a nice memory for them all, I mean – they never met him.'

'Yeah, and then we have the cousins!' They both laughed out loud.

There was a brief silence.

'Okay, I will take pictures and make an album online. We can choose the ones we want, what do you think?' Suddenly determined, Celia pulled off the dusty old scarf and shook her head. Feeling a bit fresher now, she looked at herself in the mirror and pulled a brush through her short blonde hair.

'Good idea, Sis. And don't forget to write down the measurements!'

She put the receiver down. The clinking sound echoed in the silent cottage, and she slid down to the floor. She sat there for a while with her back against the cold wall until, suddenly shivering, she rose and revived the fire. Dusk fell and she lit a candle. With her knees tucked up under the chin, she waited for the rooms to warm up again.

*

It was a peaceful and still morning in the village. The cattle had been awake since sunrise. The cows and the calves, the hens and their chickens, pottering and kicking in the stables, were happy to be protected from the cold dragging mist in the fields outside.

The sound of a pickup passing cut the silence. Celia watched it slow down a little. Its driver leaned over the passenger seat to get a better look at Celia's BMW, which was parked in front of the cottage. Built on a hill and overlooking the village, the cottage was shielded against the constant wind from the sea by four high birches and a big abandoned barn at the back. The barn was plain grey, but in the sunshine it changed its colour to silver. It was leaning, threatening to fall over every time a storm moved in. Its decay had been slow and gradual; somewhere within was a tough structure which had resisted time and change. Yet now the roof had collapsed on the north side and the distance between the planks grew broader every year.

Celia, sheltered against the cold morning air in a black puffer jacket, walked briskly on the grassy path that led from the barn towards the cottage. Holger's pale face loomed in the pickup cab and she could see his thin lips moving. Probably he was muttering to himself, thinking that these town people like to show off with big cars and fancy clothes, while they neglect the cottage and refuse to see the work that they really should be doing. She saw the man sniff in his usual way, shift gear and the pickup started to move away. The farmer lifted his hand and greeted her as he passed.

*

Celia could not believe her luck when the bleak sun suddenly won the battle and fought its way through the heavy clouds. Thankful for the perfect light, she took her heavy camera bag outside and mounted the Canon on the tripod before she started to carry the paintings down, one by one, from the cold attic. She placed some of them carefully in the yellow, dead grass, and leaned the others against the barn door or its grey silky walls. She carried them around, exploring the most advantageous settings and light. She hung paintings on rusty old nails that she randomly hammered into the wall of the barn; others she hung in trees or leaned against a trunk or a twisted bush.

As she worked, she measured them and noted the titles that Walt had written on the back. As the work progressed she got more and more absorbed by the installation itself, of the paintings placed in the roughness of nature.

She took two photographs of each one of them. One shot with her iPhone, matching it with the name and size, and one more with her high-pixel camera.

When she had finished, she sat down on a rock and flipped through the images on the display, occasionally deleting one. Sipping a cup of hot tea, she watched the light change on the lengthy grey wall, shimmering softly like velvet. And suddenly she saw the photograph.

She took out her extreme wide-angle lens and, to make sure that she would take one single perfect shot, she took a hundred.

Ben Gareh
Turkish Coffee

Mum called up the stairs. 'They will be here any minute, Berin, come down.'

I stood in front of the mirror, armed with the eyeliner she had bought for me. I had never been into make-up. My friends at university had tried giving me tips, but it just felt uncomfortable. I put the pen down and closed my eyes as the bile churned up my stomach.

'Berin, will you get down here.' My mum's voice was anger blending into panic. I couldn't stall any longer. 'Coming, Mum,' I said.

When I got to the kitchen she was arched over the stove, fiddling with a cooking pot.

'Finally,' she said, spinning round. Her eyes drifted over me before falling away. 'You look beautiful.'

'Whatever, Mum. So, have you seen him?'

She gave me one of her exasperated looks. 'Hüseyin is a good man.'

'How can you know that?' I said, wondering what her, or Baba's, definition of a good man actually was.

Mum turned back to the cooking pot.

'He's probably twice my age,' I said, staring into Mum's back, but she remained a statue. I had run out of ideas to convince her that this was wrong. Sometimes I tried to convince myself that she was just caught up in a tradition that she thought was for the best, but deep down I knew it was because she was afraid of Baba.

I looked up and there he was in the doorway with his black eyes and short bulldog frame.

'I see you got her to come down,' he said in a voice that was like a rumbling volcano.

A cup clinked as Mum brushed it with her hand. 'Yes. I told you not to worry.' She turned around and I caught her biting her lip. 'Doesn't she look nice?'

As she said the words I felt sick. I hated her for being so weak and yet what was I doing? Where was my strength?

'She looks fine.' Deep lines appeared on Baba's forehead as he spoke.

I nodded in appreciation and looked to the floor. 'What if I don't like him?' I said, before cursing myself for letting the words slip out.

'What did you say?' said Baba.

I glanced back towards Mum but she had turned round. I could see a thin plume of steam from the pot drifting up over her head.

'Nothing, Baba.' I stared at the black shoes that he had shined especially for today.

'You are lucky that I found someone suitable for you. Don't mess it up.'

The shoes waited for a response but when I didn't give one he sniffed and left the kitchen.

I watched Mum reach up and bring down the special coffee cups and saucers from the cupboard. They were the ones they had bought back from their first Hajj. Mum had been desperate to go on the sacred pilgrimage to Mecca for as long as I could remember, but Baba had never wanted to, and then, two years ago, my older brother Osman had died and the following autumn, they went.

I felt tears welling up behind my eyes but I clenched my fists and forced them back. I still missed Osman so much. He had always stood up for me where Baba was concerned and he was the only person Baba seemed to respect or listen to.

Mum placed a hand on my shoulder. 'I never had a choice with your father. That is how it was done.'

The finality of her words bought me back to the present. Would this be it? One meeting? One cup of Turkish coffee? One man? I searched my mind for an alternative scenario. Had I ever even been in love before? There was that waiter in Izmir, when I was sixteen, who bought me a rose, and kissed me on the cheek. It made my stomach flutter but that was all. Luckily, Baba had never seen it but Osman knew. I told him. Then there was Nick at uni who was always so nice to me despite the fact that our cultures were worlds apart. I would have loved to be able to tell Osman about him. To ask his advice.

I felt a tear of frustration trickle down the side of my face. My mother saw it, wiped it with her thumb and cupped my cheeks with her warm hands. 'My darling, please don't be sad. We only want what's best for you.'

'But, Mum,' I said trying to steady my voice. 'What about love?'

She glanced to the side and took a deep breath. 'True love is not just about what you read in books, Berin.'

I noticed something in the corner of her eye which caught the light and glittered.

'Mum, do you truly love Baba?'

Her eyes shot back at me. 'Times were different then. Our heads weren't filled with all this silly stuff. I had a duty to my father the same way you do.'

'You mean to do what he says.'

'To respect him, Berin.'

'I do respect him.' I stared at her, pleading.

'I know, my darling, but you have to understand it is how we do things.'

'I don't know if I can, Mum.'

She looked at the floor for a moment, 'I know you think love is like what you see in the movies, but you will learn that it is not.'

The numbness began to creep out from my stomach into my limbs again. I felt trapped in this kitchen, this house.

'Nobody really falls in love straight away. That is just lust, and lust will always fade.'

I felt myself shaking. 'No, Mum. That is not right.' My sight was foggy with tears and I could feel them burning my cheeks but I held her gaze. 'Maybe you accept this. Maybe you can block your emotions, but I can't and I won't.'

My heart was pumping fast and a burning heat swept through my body, shooting into my hands and feet. I pulled away from her and ran up the stairs and into my room, throwing myself on to the bed and burying my head in the pillow. I was so angry but I was also scared. I did believe that Mum felt some unbreakable sense of duty to Baba. But love? That was different. Her perspective was warped, it came out of the old school where emotions were hidden away from view like a nasty scar or an oversized birthmark. Most of my family had indeed met each other this way. I was different though. I had been schooled in England. I loved books. I watched English films and tweeted with my friends. Many of the older women in my family, the ones from the village back in Turkey, couldn't even read.

I lay there, my face wet with tears. I could hear the muffled voices of my parents floating up from below and then just my baba shouting. I heard him clumping up the stairs and I squeezed my eyes tight and clenched my fists. The footsteps came closer and stopped outside my room. Downstairs, the doorbell rang.

I heard his shoes shuffling behind the door before working their way back down the stairs. That was close. The front door clicked open. 'Hoş Geldiniz.' My mum's voice was welcoming and soft, betraying nothing.

I lifted my head up and turning on to my side I reached for a tissue. I wondered how my mum put up with him.

An awkward silence drifted up from the living room in the form of the odd polite cough. I wondered if I was overreacting. Maybe he would be nice, good-looking even. Maybe he wasn't that old. I knew Mum would be ashamed if I didn't come down and serve the coffee. How would they explain where I was? My baba would die of embarrassment. He would want to strangle me.

I sat up on the bed and took a deep breath. Maybe I should go and meet them. Get it out of the way. I mean it wasn't as if they were going to marry me off there and then – and what if I actually liked him? I got out of bed and forced myself to look in the mirror. My eyes were puffy and my cheeks were red, but at least there were no tracks of mascara. I pulled off my dark green headscarf and shook my black curls free. It felt good to see them, almost empowering. I wanted to go downstairs like that and confront all of them. I wanted to tell them that I would not marry someone I didn't love, someone that I barely knew.

I could hear another set of footsteps creeping up the stairs, lighter ones. I wrapped the scarf back round my head and tucked in the loose tufts of hair. I wondered if Mum had ever felt as if she had wanted to break out. Even for a moment.

There was a knock on the door. 'Berin, please open the door.' Her voice was low and strained.

When I came out and saw her standing on the landing, I

thought she looked smaller than I had ever seen her. 'Please, Berin, can you come down and help me serve the coffee?'

'What's he like?' I said.

She took my hand and squeezed it, but avoided my eyes. 'Come,' she said.

She led me downstairs and as I entered the sitting room I could feel my heart thumping against my chest. I took a brief glance round the room. There were three people. An old man with a heavily wrinkled face and thinning white hair was sitting next to a gaunt woman with protruding eyes which immediately began to examine me. I turned to the third guest who was an overweight middle-aged man with a bushy moustache and black slicked-back hair. He looked like one of the bad guys from the old movies that Mum loved to watch on Turkish television. I felt his beady eyes crawling all over me while an ugly smile appeared on his lips. It made my skin crawl and I began to lose feeling in my legs. Was this the man who Baba expected me to spend the rest of my life with?

'Berin, this is Hüseyin and his aunt and uncle. They have come to meet you,' said Baba.

I nodded and prayed for Mum to drag me into the kitchen. My throat felt as though it was filling up with sand.

'Merhaba,' said a deep voice.

'This is my daughter Berin,' said Baba.

'Merhaba. Hoş Geldiniz,' I said, looking at the floor.

'Come, Berin, let's bring the coffee.' My mum led me away into the kitchen where I slumped into a chair.

Mum's wrinkled hand touched my face. 'You look grey, Berin. Are you okay?'

I tried to force some words out through my heavy breathing and pounding chest but nothing came, so I just shook my head.

Mum poured me a glass of water and helped me sip it. She rubbed my back and told me to take deep breaths. I began to feel calmer and the beating against my chest subsided, but the panic only gave way to a deep sadness.

When she looked at me I could see my heartache reflecting back out of her moist grey eyes, but she didn't say any more, she just left me at the table while she laid the china cups in a line and prepared the coffee in the pot on the stove. I watched her small hands carefully spooning the froth into the bottom of each cup before filling them to the top. She arranged the baklava the guests had brought on a plate and placed it along with the coffee cups on a tray. When she had finished, she turned and looked at me and I forced myself out of the chair.

Mum shuffled around with the tray, gesturing for me to serve the coffee and sweets. We served the old man and woman first and then she stopped in front of Hüseyin. As I handed him the cup, his thumb brushed my hand and I felt sick. I didn't want to look up, but I could feel his eyes undressing me. I turned to take the last cup off the tray to serve Baba and I noticed that Mum was staring at Hüseyin as he sipped his drink. I could see that she was making him feel uncomfortable as he shifted in his seat. 'Delicious coffee, Ayşe Teyze,' he said.

I took Baba's cup and Mum took the tray back to the kitchen. I sat down on one of the dining chairs that Mum had placed on either side of the television. One for her and one for me.

'So. Your father tells me you are attending university,' said Hüseyin, His voice was as oily as his hair.

'Yes. I am studying English.'

'She wants to be a teacher.' Mum's voice was laced with determination as she sat down next to me. I had to look at her twice. Baba narrowed his eyes.

Hüseyin's uncle gave a disapproving cough. The idea of a Turkish woman doing anything but bringing up children and cooking dinner for her family was probably quite alien to him.

'Hüseyin has got two restaurants, Ayşe. I don't think that any wife of his would have to work.' Baba turned from Mum to the uncle, who gave him an affirmatory nod.

'That is very nice,' said Mum as she continued to stare straight at Hüseyin.

The aunt began tucking into the baklava as though her life depended on it while her husband sipped his coffee.

The creases in Baba's forehead were deepening by the second and I feared for the outburst that Mum and I would be subjected to once they had left. 'So how is business, Hüseyin?' he said after some consideration.

'Business is good.'

I watched Baba take his final sip of coffee before I rushed off to fetch the tray and collect the empty cups.

The guests didn't stay much longer and when they had left I disappeared into the kitchen and sat down. A few moments later I was joined by Mum. 'What was the matter with you, Mum? Why were you staring at Hüseyin like that?'

She stood in front of me, and for the first time in two years I saw the fire in her eyes that had been missing for so long. 'Are you interested in this man?'

'Mum?'

'Do you want to see him again?'

'No, Mum. I don't want to see him again.'

Before Mum had a chance to say anything else, Baba threw open the door. 'What is going on, Ayşe?'

Mum turned around. I could see that she had made fists with both her hands. 'She doesn't want him, Abdullah. And we cannot make her do what she doesn't want?'

Baba slammed his fist into the wall. 'What are you talking about, woman? He will take care of her.'

'She can take care of herself, Abdullah. She is not weak.'

'She is a girl. A daughter, not a son. A daughter doesn't take care of herself.'

I looked up at Baba. His face was beetroot. His eyes were like the devil. I was sure he was going to beat us to death. I had never heard my mother speak to him like this before.

'Osman is dead, Abdullah, but we still have a daughter and this daughter can take care of herself.' Mum's head didn't move, it stayed in the same position as Baba's eyes darted between her and me. He stepped towards us, his hands curling into hammers and I felt the adrenalin course through me. I stood up next to Mum and we both stared at him together.

He stopped in front of us and clamped my cheeks between his hands like a vice, pulling them towards him. 'I am your father and you will do what I say.' His face was compressed into a grimace as though he could feel the pain he was inflicting.

Mum grabbed his arm but he just swatted her away and she fell backwards on to the table. The force of her weight shook the tray of cups and one of them tumbled off the edge and fell on to the floor, shattering on impact. We all turned to look and Baba released the pressure of his hands on my face.

Three cups remained huddled together on the corner of the tray, which was balancing over the table. I pulled myself away and grabbed Mum.

'Look at what you've done,' said Baba, but this time his eyes weren't jet black and his tone didn't shake the room.

Mum took a deep breath and stooped down to pick up the fractured pieces of china. I moved the tray and bent over to help her.

Baba's shiny shoes slowly turned and left the kitchen. We heard him trudge upstairs and shut a bedroom door. Mum placed the china pieces into a plastic bag and lowered it into the bin. I washed the other cups and set them on the side to dry.

A hand gently pressed itself on to my back and it felt as though it was drawing out all the negative emotion. I closed my eyes and imagined it was my brother's hand and that he would turn me round and tell me it was okay and that he would go upstairs and talk to Baba. It slid up my shoulder and gently pulled. I opened my eyes and stared through the fog of tears. I saw my Mum's wrinkled face in front of me but then I noticed something for the first time. The eyes that stared up at me were Osman's eyes.

Lizzy Barber
Café

Tel Aviv, 1941

The air hummed with voices.

To Cecile, it seemed as if the entire population of Tel Aviv had spilled out to enjoy itself on the beach promenade. A noisy, jostling hubbub; a melting pot of Moroccan Sephardis and Polish Hassidics and German intellectuals and Sabra aristocrats and children and mothers and soldiers and sun and sand and pride. This was the old, new land. This was 'The First Hebrew City': a city built on a lottery of sea shells. And it culminated here, on Allenby Road, in the smart cafés, hotels and restaurants filled with the Beautiful People. Here Cecile sat, head thrown back into the sun, deliberately flouting her white parasol.

Café Pinati was proud of its reputation as a hot spot among the young and wealthy of Tel Aviv. Centrally located, flanked by palm trees and boasting the guarantee that 'our cake is home-made, and we only use real butter,' it was the perfect place to offer respite from the fierce heat and the hordes on the beach. But now it had taken on a new and even more fascinating significance: it was a favoured watering spot of the British officers. And where there were British officers, there were flocks of young women.

Shoshanna, sitting beside her, sighed. 'Oh, Ceecee, I wish you wouldn't do that. My mother says that tans are vulgar.' Shoshanna was always overly concerned with doing the Right Thing. Cecile had tolerated her since she had returned from boarding school three months ago largely because Shoshanna eventually tended to do whatever she said.

Cecile rolled her eyes inwardly as she pressed a handkerchief to her sticky neck.

'Oh, Shoshanna please stop quoting your mother at me. In the words of Coco Chanel, "a girl simply has to tan."' She pulled out the spare chair next to her and propped up her feet. She knew that Shoshanna wouldn't argue. One never could with Chanel.

Cecile watched languidly as Shoshanna twisted in her seat, trying to get a good view of the cluster of uniformed men taking seats by the entrance to the café. They chatted loudly, jostled about and beckoned to the waiter. One man was slightly apart from the rest, and she found herself catching his eye. She reddened, and quickly turned away, but not before Shoshanna noticed.

'Ceecee,' she whispered, moving in closer. 'That man is staring at you.' Cecile tried to appear nonchalant as she took in the tall figure with the shock of blond hair who was now unashamedly gazing at her.

'Mmm . . . ' she shrugged, and went back to drinking her lemonade. Shoshanna huffed and turned back to one of the women's magazines her cousin in New York sent over and she routinely devoured. An article in last month's Mademoiselle titled 'How to Make the Most of your Marriage' had nearly sent her over the edge. Cecile never took any interest in these articles, no matter how many Shoshanna tried to impress on her. Cecile could tell Shoshanna was close to retrieving another one from her handbag and looked eagerly around for a distraction. She sighed as a waiter approached their table.

'Excuse me, ladies, I have been asked to give this to the young lady from the gentleman over there.' And he handed Cecile a small slip of paper which appeared to have been torn from a notebook. Cecile glanced over to where the waiter was pointing, and saw a blond head peeking surreptitiously over the top of a newspaper. He smiled behind the paper; the boys had put him up to it, and he wasn't one to say no to a challenge. She gently unfurled the note.

Do you speak English?

Cecile smiled and took a pen out of her bag, writing neatly and carefully one word on the back: *Yes*. Placing the lid back on the pen with a satisfied click, she refolded the paper and handed it back to the waiter.

'Would you be so kind as to return this?'

A minute later he was back, and she noticed a film of sweat forming over his thin moustache. The café was full, and she supposed the Bright Young Things of Tev Aviv weren't known for their patience. Again Cecile unfolded the note.

You are very beautiful.

The hand was large and flowing; an artistic hand which seemed at odds with the military garb of its possessor. Once again she searched for her pen and turned the note to write on the back.

I know.

Only this time she thanked and dismissed the waiter, folded the paper into the shape of an aeroplane and aimed it straight for the officer, feeling the tip of her tongue poking out of her mouth as she honed her aim. The paper landed squarely in his hair, and his companions burst out laughing as he fished it out. His laughter joined the rest once he had opened it and read her reply. Cecile, secretly delighted with herself and still determined to appear casual, lit up a cigarette and leaned back in her chair, angling it ever so slightly to observe her pursuer in her peripheral vision.

She was unsurprised when Shoshanna merely sighed and called

for a second lemonade without touching the cigarette packet on the table. The week after Cecile had returned to Tel Aviv they had gone to see *Philadelphia Story* at the Eden Cinema and she had decided that they needed to learn to smoke more like Katherine Hepburn. She had made them each smoke an entire pack of Lucky Strikes in the mirror until they looked the part, and Shoshanna had been sick on Cecile's white bedroom carpet. She hadn't touched a cigarette since.

The sound of a throat being cleared made both girls turn around, and they saw the officer standing behind them.

'Oh, hello there.' Cecile's voice came out a notch higher-pitched than she had anticipated. He was taller close up.

He doffed his cap and gave a shallow bob.

'I came to thank you for your aeroplane. It is rather smaller than the ones I've been in, but I assure you it is no less well built.' He extended his hand. 'Captain David Saunders.'

His English was rounded and melodic, and she hoped hers didn't sound thick and clumsy in comparison. Slowly she took a drag of her cigarette, watching the thin stream of smoke curl and evaporate, and summoned her best Received Pronunciation.

'Very young to be a Captain. Are you sure?'

'Ceecee!' Shoshanna hissed, digging her elbow into Cecile's ribs. 'I do apologise, Captain Saunders,' she beamed at him. 'The heat seems to have got the better of my friend. Captain, this is Cecile Misrahi, and I am Shoshanna Sana.'

'Pleased to meet you both.' He shook both their hands with a firm, masculine grip. 'I can understand the effect of the heat, I assure you. It's sweltering today.' He faced Cecile. 'And in answer to your question, Miss Misrahi, yes, I am sure. And if not, someone should probably inform the chaps who keep on following my orders.'

Cecile allowed herself the freedom of a laugh, and her eyes met Captain Saunders, who smiled at her.

'In truth, Miss Sana, Miss Misrahi, I think a university degree and the decision to draft early may have helped somewhat.'

'Oh, a university degree, Captain Saunders? How wonderful.' Shoshanna raised her eyes pointedly at Cecile, who wished she would be a little less obvious. 'Do sit down and have a drink with us. The café is famous for its lemonade.'

'Actually, ladies, I'm afraid we're about to head on our way, but I was actually wondering if by any chance you enjoyed dancing?'

'Oh, yes.' Shoshanna cried at once. 'We love to dance. We practise together all the time. Foxtrot, Swing, Rumba, Carioca, Continental . . . '

'Why do you ask?' Cecile cut in smoothly, and saw Shoshanna clamp her mouth shut, finally embarrassed. The officer's eyes twinkled as he watched the exchange

'Well, I'm sure you have a whole host of things to do tonight, but a group of us boys are planning on heading over to Bar-Kokhba tonight. We hear it's "the place to be" around here. We'd certainly love to have you girls as our guests.'

Before Shoshanna could open her mouth, Cecile gave a loud, thoughtful miaow.

'Mmm . . . yes, Bar-Kokhba, we go there all the time.' She smiled up at David as sweetly as she could. 'We did have a few plans, but I'm sure we could rearrange some things, couldn't we, Shoshie?'

Shoshanna nodded dumbly.

'Well, that's wonderful. We plan to be there about nine, if that would suit you?'

'That sounds perfect, Captain Saunders. We shall see you there at nine.'

'Please, call me David.' He bent down, took her fingertips lightly in his right hand, and kissed her softly on the back of her palm. 'And I look forward to it.' With a nod of his head towards Shoshanna, who was now rendered speechless, he went back to join his companions.

When they had left, Shoshanna turned to Cecile, her eyes bulging.

'Ceecee,' she squawked. 'Why on earth did you say we go to the Bar-Kokhba *all the time*? We've *never* been there. I'm not *allowed* to go there. My mother will have a fit. She says it's *not at all nice*. She says it's full of low-lifes. And besides – '

'Oh, do calm down, Shoshanna,' Cecile replied calmly, lighting another cigarette. 'You're to tell your mother you're staying with me. And you know my mother will be too preoccupied with Uncle Max to notice whether we're in the house or not. And besides, you have to come tonight – ' She lowered her voice mysteriously. ' – I thought I noticed one of David's pals making eyes at you . . . '

Shoshanna turned pink. 'Really? Which one? The one with the brown hair? Or the thin one with the moustache? I thought I saw the one with the moustache looking at me, but he may have just been squinting in the sun. Was it him?'

'I'm not quite sure . . . you'll have to find out tonight . . . ' She took an indulgent sip of lemonade, but couldn't help feeling a flutter of excitement. Captain David Saunders. Bar-Kokhba. Not bad for an ordinary Sunday at the beach.

Kate Weinberg
An Arrival

The only event from my childhood that it occurs to me to mention happened during the Easter holidays. I was ten or maybe eleven at the time. Milton View was set back from a busy road on a bumpy track that led over a hill to a farm that was part arable, part sheep. I know it was Easter because the pregnant sheep had been taken from the surrounding fields and placed in a large corrugated iron barn at the back of the farm. Despite having grown up next door, I'd never actually been present at a lambing. Newborn lambs can pass on a rare but terrible disease to unborn children called toxoplasmosis. As a midwife who had witnessed the arrival of several babies with birth defects, my mother was taking no chances. The barn was off limits during lambing season, even after her fourth and final pregnancy with the twins was long and safely over.

That morning, though, I was on my own. This was not as much of an unusual occurrence as you might think in a large family. My elder sister and brother naturally teamed up as did the twins below me. As a result, I was pretty self-sufficient, at least in a superficial sense. It was a hazy, hay-fevery day with great bits of white fluff drifting through the air. My eyes and nose itched relentlessly as I walked up the rutted track that led to the barn, hoping for some kind of event to separate this day from the next three weeks of school holidays which yawned ahead.

Hay fever, if you've never had it, is a much underrated hardship. Fire ants crawl up into your nostrils and round the backs of your eyeballs and it feels as if someone has left the taps running in every room of your body. I was much shorter than average as a child, with a square haircut and fringe that I now consider a low move by my mother. I remember swinging my arms wildly as I walked, as if I could disperse the pollen from the air.

Even from a distance, I could hear the noises coming from the barn – the low baaing of adult sheep punctuated by the insistent bleats of very new lambs. It sounded as if different sections of an orchestra were tuning up inside.

I quickened my step, enough of a country child to sense something out of the ordinary was happening. Inside the barn, it was shady and cool, a relief to my streaming eyes. I walked past several stalls, some only occupied by single ewes, their bellies swollen with late pregnancy, others with ewes standing protectively over their newborns, rolling their milky, marble eyes. The smell of urine-soaked straw was strong. It wasn't until I was halfway into the cavernous space, admiring the tiny perfection of the new lambs on their tottering legs, waving their tails frantically as they tugged at their mother's teats, that I heard low human voices mingling with the sheep noises. Farmer Roberts was leaning against the side of a pen, talking softly but urgently to his daughter, who was kneeling down next to a sheep inside.

I was a little scared of Farmer Roberts, for the very good reason that he only had half a face. The other half was made of what looked like, and I think probably was, badly glued-down pieces of pink plastic surrounding a glass eye. The story was, as my older brother once gleefully related, that he had tried to blow his brains out with a rifle but had missed and blown a hole through his cheek instead. We had taken bets as to the reason: my older brother Freddie thought it was because his wife was sleeping around. Celia, the intellectual, thought it was because the European Union didn't pay him enough of a stipend and the twins, a little confused, thought it was because he was upset at only having half a face.

Farmer Roberts' daughter, who at the time I thought of as a grown-up but was probably only in her mid to late teens, was a scary girl called Helen. Helen was a blonde with dark roots who always wore dirty jeans and zipper tops and rarely smiled. She was not smiling now as she kneeled at the back end of an ewe who was lying down in the pen, emitting low sounds like someone straining to clear a very painful throat. Below the ewe's tail there was a large bloodstained patch in the straw.

I was approaching Farmer Roberts on his bad side. He was so busy talking to his daughter that it took him a while to notice me. When he finally did, he lifted his head briefly and said curtly, 'Stay back please,' before continuing to address Helen in a soft, persuasive voice that was very different from the grunt he usually used if he saw us wandering about the farm.

'Okay, it's a breech, Helen, so you're going to need to give her some help. Put some more soap on your hand. Okay, now slide it in very gently so you can feel what's going on . . . '

I watched rapt and a little disgusted as Helen pushed her hand inside, her forehead shiny pink with effort. The ewe writhed some more, her sides lifting and falling like bellows. Then she made a sort of barking sound, and a pink sheath appeared out of her backside containing a grey filmy balloon with what looked like a tiny pair of hooves inside.

'Keep her steady now, she's almost there.'

The sheep gave out a low guttural groan which provoked another chorus of baas from the sheep and lambs in the nearby stalls. There was a sticky, rushing sound, and the lamb's back legs began to slither out on to the straw. I felt excitement and nerves balling up in my chest and caught the shiny gaze of triumph in Helen's eyes. Something, I'm not sure what, made me glance over at Farmer Roberts. The good side of his mouth was set in a grim line and I only had a half second to wonder why before Helen gave a great tug, the sheep's sides contracted again and there was a dull popping sound. It should have been the head of the lamb. Except there wasn't any head, just a stump. It must have snapped off, caught between the pulling and the contractions. In that grotesque frozen second, I saw it in my mind's eye, left swilling around inside the ewe's belly. Or perhaps, I thought, the head had just never grown in the first place.

The ewe struggled to her feet and moved away from her deformed stillborn.

I had time to glimpse the stunned expression on Helen's face and the still look on Farmer Roberts', and then I was outside the barn, running, running, running, back to Milton View where nothing exciting ever happened but nothing terrible either.

When I got back to the house, my brothers and sisters were in the middle of playing Kick the Can, so I never told them. Nor did I tell my dad, who I knew, with a child's intuition, never wanted to hear anything bad, nor my mother who could take all the bad things in the world in her stride but would never comfort me.

In fact I'm not even sure why I'm telling you, except for the fact that when I think about it now, the horror rises in me still, and I wonder what it was in that moment that I lost.

Stuart McLean
Mad Dog

Chapter 1

Most important thing in this job, Jack was telling him, is make sure you always answer the bloody phone. 'Management have a habit of checking up on us, phoning up at weird times just to make sure we're not asleep, or buggered off down the pub. You can get up to whatever the hell you want in here, just make sure to answer the phone, right?'

'Right.'

Dog squirmed inside his uniform. It felt at least two sizes too small. Every time he moved, the fabric tugged at his chest, or gripped way too tightly around his thighs. The seams were almost stretched to breaking point. It was only a matter of time before something gave way.

His uniform was the only thing in the security cabin that looked new. Everything else was out of date, broken down or just plain old. The two plastic swivel chairs had several rips in the upholstery with clumps of brown foam rubber poking through. They squeaked loudly in protest every time he sat down. In the corner of the cabin was a kettle and two mugs, stained with years of limescale. A cool breeze occasionally wafted in through the open doorway, pausing to ruffle Dog's hair, before making its escape through a hole in the cracked windowpane. A television clung to the wall, held on by a rusting metal bracket. Grainy black-and-white images played on the screen. Every thirty seconds or so the image would change, as it cycled through a rota of CCTV camera views. Underneath the television was a black console, lined with a series of thick plastic buttons. Stale cigarette smoke seemed to coat his lungs every time he breathed.

Like everything else in the cabin, Dog's supervisor was ancient and decrepit. Jack was a white-haired relic, with wrinkled leathery skin and bloodshot eyes. He wore false teeth that would roam around inside his mouth whenever he spoke, breaking up his speech and making him sound as if he was drunk. He was dressed in a blue security guard's uniform, almost identical to Dog's, except that Jack's was old and ragged. Should be in a museum, thought Dog, have some lab-rat carbon-date it for posterity. The uniform and the man.

'One other thing you need to know,' Jack slurred. 'Actually, forget what I said before, this is the most important thing of all. In fact, you might want to write this one down.'

'Yes?'

Jack nodded towards the kettle. 'I take two sugars in my tea.'

Dog took the hint.

A few minutes later he sat back on the chair – still creaking its dissent – and handed over a steaming mug to Jack. Dog rested his own cup on his lap.

The television screen flickered. An image of the main factory entrance appeared: a pair of heavy wrought-iron gates hung in the gap between two brick walls. Several lengths of barbed wire spiralled along the top of each wall.

'So what did you do before?' Jack paused to blow wetly on his tea. 'Y'know, before you wound up in this dump?'

'Bit of this, bit of that. Stacked shelves in a supermarket for a while, drove a minicab . . . '

'You in a minicab? Shit, must've been a bloody big 'un.'

Dog smiled. 'Yeah. I've also worked as a bodyguard, did a stint as a bouncer in a nightclub, delivered parcels. All sorts, really. Basically, I'm a factotum.'

'A facto-what?'

'Factotum. Like, someone who does a load of different jobs.'

'Jeez, why didn't you say that in the first place, 'stead of giving me your bloody Welsh mumbo-jumbo.'

The television screen flickered once more. The image changed to show the rear of the plant where a gravel road ran alongside the factory wall. Parallel to the road was an area of wasteland; knee-high grass grew in random clumps amidst rocky terrain. A white van had parked in the road. Dog could see two men leaning against the side of the vehicle. Despite the heat, they wore sweatshirts with hoods pulled forward, obscuring their faces.

'What's going on there?' asked Dog.

One of the hoodies went to the back of the van, swung the doors wide open. Then the image changed. There was a brief flicker and the gravel road disappeared, replaced by an image of an office block.

'Damn it,' said Dog. 'How do we get back to the previous shot?'

Jack didn't move. He took a long casual slurp from his tea. 'Relax, it's just kids.'

'I want to see.'

Jack reached over to the console and jabbed half-heartedly at a green button. The image of the van reappeared on the television screen. The two men were now leaning against the bonnet. Their hoods were still pulled low, their hands buried deep in their pockets, trying to look casual.

'Told you, it's just kids,' said Jack. 'Druggies, probably. They hang round there sometimes. Don't worry, they ain't going to bother us none.'

A third man came into view, entering from the edge of the screen and approaching the van. He wore baggy clothes and walked with a swagger, one arm swinging like a pendulum. Seen too many rap videos, thought Dog.

The other two men greeted the newcomer with high fives and handshakes. One of the hoodies went to the back of the van, emerging with something clenched in his fist. There was an exchange; a brief surreptitious joining of hands as something was passed over from one to another.

'What do we do?' asked Dog. 'Call the police?'

Jack snorted. 'What for? All they'll do is chase the buggers off, make 'em sell their stuff somewhere else. Ah, just leave them. Long as they don't come over that wall, it's no business of ours.'

No business of ours, thought Dog. Sod that. He got up from the chair and walked out of the security cabin.

'Hey, feller, where you goin'?' Jack shouted after him. 'I told you it's nothin' worth bothering about.'

Dog walked out through the factory gates. He followed the pavement towards the rear of the factory, walking with a relaxed easy stroll. He rounded the corner. The three men were still there.

The two hoodies leaned casually against the van, their faces barely visible beneath the hoods. They were young, probably in their late teens. The third man was even younger, couldn't have been more than fifteen. Not even old enough to purchase a pack of cigarettes, let alone buy whatever crap these guys were selling him.

One of the hoodies glanced over. 'Copper,' he said.

The other one just laughed. 'Relax, it's just one of them security guards.'

Dog walked over, keeping his hands loose, his arms swinging gently. 'Hey, lads,' he said. 'How's it going?'

'Fuck you.'

Charming, thought Dog. 'So, er, what's going on here then, lads?'

'Nothing,' said one of the hoodies. He shuffled his feet, looked down at the ground.

'Isn't there's some other place you should be?' Dog asked. 'I mean, come on, nice night like this, shouldn't you be in town? Watching girls and stuff?'

'What's it to you?' the second hoodie replied.

'It's just that I'm looking after the factory, here. And, seeing you guys hanging around, it makes me a bit nervous. So, I was wondering if maybe you'd consider moving on. Just as a favour to me, like. Know what I'm saying?'

The three men looked at one another and burst into laughter. One of the hoodies slapped the other one on the back. 'He wants us to move on,' the man giggled.

'I'm serious,' said Dog.

'Ah, piss off. None of your business where we hang out.'

Dog took a step forwards. 'Maybe. Or, maybe I'm making it my business.'

'Oh yeah? What you gonna do?'

Dog took another step forwards, moving towards the back of the van. He grabbed the door handle.

'What the fuck?' One of the hoodies pulled something from his pocket. He came around the van. A knife, six inches of ugly serrated metal, extended towards Dog's face. 'Get away from there,' the man said.

'Ah, now, there's no need to be like that,' said Dog. 'I was only going to have a look.'

The man moved closer.

'Go on, Lee,' said the other hoodie. 'Cut him.'

Dog raised his hand, palms outwards. 'Okay, I don't want any trouble.'

Lee was getting cocky. He jabbed the knife through the air, the tip of the blade pricking at Dog's chin. 'Trouble? You got trouble all right.'

Dog moved. He grabbed Lee's wrist, twisting it hard, jerking the knife away from his face. There was a sharp crack as something snapped. Lee screamed. The knife fell from his grasp. Dog shoved him roughly to one side. Lee slumped on to the ground, cradling his wrist. 'Jesus,' he cried. 'He's broke my fuckin' arm.'

The other hoodie danced uncertainly from one foot to the other, then launched himself forwards, swinging clumsy punches at Dog's face. Dog dodged the blows, two, three times, then he threw a punch of his own, directing it squarely in the centre of the man's face. It connected perfectly. His nose sprayed blood. The hoodie staggered back, a stunned expression on his face. Then he dropped on to his backside and groaned.

The third man wasn't quite so brave. He turned on his heels and tried to run. Dog was quicker. He chased the man across the wasteland for a few hundred yards, finally bringing him down with a rugby tackle, his arms around the man's waist.

'You,' said Dog, pinning him to the ground. 'What've you bought? Come on, whatever you've got, hand it over.'

The man squirmed. Dog shook him by the collar. The man reached into the pocket of his jeans and pulled out a small object, wrapped in tinfoil. He handed it over.

'Now, get out of here. And don't come back. Spread the word, these guys are no longer in business.'

Dog stood up. The man scrambled to his feet and ran, tripping over the undergrowth as he disappeared into the darkness. Dog went back towards the van. Lee was on his knees, cradling his arm and moaning loudly. 'Jesus, my arm.'

The other man was sitting on the ground, holding his sleeve against his nose, mopping up blood. He flinched when Dog approached, grabbed him by the scruff of his neck and dragged him to his feet.

'What's your name, son?' he asked.

'Carl.'

'Okay, Carl. Open the van. Show me what's in there.'

Carl walked over to the van on unsteady legs. He threw the doors open. Inside, there were two cardboard boxes, each containing hundreds of small tinfoil packets. Dog picked up one of the boxes and shoved it at Carl. He tucked the second box under one arm, then he grabbed Carl's collar once again and frogmarched him to the edge of the road.

'You've broken my bloody arm,' he heard Lee cry out as they went past.

'Oh, do stop whining,' said Dog.

There was a storm drain in the gutter; a square hole covered by a rusting metal grid. Dog dropped the box at his feet, tugged at the grid. It was stuck hard, but with a sharp yank he was able to lift it away from the hole. He tossed it to one side and said to Carl, 'In there.'

'What?'

'The drugs. Throw them away.'

Carl looked at him wide-eyed. 'Jesus, you're kidding. Any idea how much this stuff is worth?'

Dog slapped him across the face. 'That feel like I'm kidding?'

'Okay, okay.' Carl opened the box. He upended the box, pouring the small metallic packets into the hole. They disappeared with a barely audible splash. Dog handed him the second box. Carl tipped the contents into the darkness.

Carl looked up, as if to say, 'What now?'

Dog took a step forwards, leaning in menacingly close, his chin inches from the man's bleeding nose.

'Now, go,' he said. 'Both of you, get out of here. And don't come back. You're not selling any more of your garbage round here, got it?'

Carl nodded. Then he spun around and ran back towards the van, pausing only to shout at Lee, 'Come on, man. Get up.'

Lee struggled to his feet, still cradling his broken arm. They climbed inside the van, not even taking the time to shut the rear doors. The tyres kicked up a spray of gravel as the van lurched forwards and sped down the road, the back doors swinging like the flippers on a pinball machine.

Dog watched the van disappear around the corner. Then he looked at his hands. They were shaking. He shook his head, marvelling at his own stupidity. What the hell had he been thinking? What if there had been more than one knife? What if one of them had been carrying something heavier? What if they had all come at him at once? There were a lot of ifs. None of them pleasant.

It wasn't even as if he'd achieved anything, not when you looked at the big picture. Sure, he'd run off a couple of pushers for one night. But Jack was right. They'd only be back tomorrow, or else selling their gear somewhere else.

He walked back towards the front of the factory, his feet dragging slowly across the pavement. The adrenaline had worn off, and all he had left was a cold feeling of emptiness. He walked through the factory gates and entered the security cabin.

Jack was staring at the television screen.

'Been watching this weird programme on telly,' he said. 'Gang of lads were hanging around, selling drugs and stuff. Then this big feller comes along, kicks the shit out of 'em all. Just like Batman. Or maybe that old feller, you know, the Equalizer. Only, it was a bit more violent. So what was all that about?' the old man asked.

'I don't like drug dealers.'

'Yeah, I noticed. No wonder they call you Mad Dog.'

Dog sat down. He reached for his tea. It was cold.

'Let me get you a fresh one,' said Jack. 'You look like you could use it.'

He shuffled towards the kettle. Dog could hear the old man faintly humming something under his breath. It sounded like the Batman theme song.

Rachel Knightley
Anything But Summertime

This was definitely her last cigarette.

Ever.

And it would be fine.

Joanna leant against the ex-church, now Café Sanctuary. She rested one platform boot on the wall, the other in a puddle, which was evaporating in the growing warmth. Lunch-hour traffic congealed on Richmond High Street. She patted the dark mess of tobacco shavings into line and rolled.

She'd get over this. It was just ritual. She didn't miss Catholicism and she wouldn't miss this. But God, the lovely silver tin. Well, she could put sweets in the tin instead of tobacco. Mints, maybe. Fruit pastilles. A new ritual. Giving up was good. Everything was fine.

What the fuck was that tapping? Shit. Her own foot. *Ode to fucking Joy.* She kicked the church wall. The bloody piped, tinkly music Laurence had been playing. Why hadn't his mysterious fucking pianist turned up? It was sacrilege to play that mental candyfloss in a church – or ex-church.

Her lips pressed the filter paper, felt the sticking point of her lipstick forming a last purple kiss. She hadn't even lit it and could already feel the reassuring fire in her chest, the burn and quick relief of that safe little hunger. She fished in the hole in the lining of her coat, where the silver lighter always dropped through the pocket. So this was it: she'd prepared the body of her last cigarette. Life as she knew it, fourteen years . . .

Except it wasn't fourteen years, was it? She'd just pretended long enough to forget it wasn't true. It was eighteen years. Joanna had been smoking since she was twelve.

It was easy to believe the official version. Her parents never asked because they couldn't complain, not on twenty a day. Abigail had assumed the reason her best friend smelt of Silk Cut was her best friend's parents smelt of Silk Cut. Not a chance. Joanna was a smoker. The cigarette she'd snatched out of Daniel Moore's hand in the playground, wiping the smirk off that beautiful bastard's face, that was just the coming-out party.

And this was the funeral. She cupped a hand to shield the flame from the drizzly breeze, and flicked.

Stop!

Something caught her eye dead opposite, outside the charity shop. The street was full of people, pushing into shops against people pushing out, moving too quickly to notice anything other than themselves. No, wait, there was something. Stillness. Blue, behind the movement. Electric blue, almost the exact shade of her own hair.

The gap in the crowd grew wider. There, briefly, was a face that was fixed on hers. A pale young woman in a blue dress, holding a hand up in what looked like a blessing, her palm flat, as if she was pressing invisible glass.

The passing crowd stayed parted, as if registering the command. The girl didn't look away, didn't blink. Her focus was absolute, unapologetic. She was the age and colouring and kindness of Our Lady. Just like the statue in Dad's church.

If this was a vision, it didn't look like a telling-off for smoking. The girl was looking at her with total, undisguised love. People didn't do that.

'Mary?' said Joanna.

'JV?'

'Shit!' She jumped at Abigail's hand on her shoulder.

Abigail jumped as Joanna jumped. 'Why did you just call me Mary?'

'That girl . . . ' She pointed across the road. But the gap in the crowd had closed, there was nothing to see but moving people. Then a break. 'Mary!' But the girl wasn't looking at Joanna any more. The 'stop' hand had been taken by a man with carrier bags, trying to give her one to hold. Joanna kicked Café Sanctuary's wall. 'Shit. No. Nothing.'

'You look like you've seen a ghost.'

'More like a vision.'

'Mazal tov. Your dad'll be thrilled.'

'Fuck off. The only thing that gets me into even this church – '

' – is the hot chocolates named after the apostles. I know, I know. So, I'll see you at rehearsal?' Abigail pushed limp ringlets off a face newly mascara-free and tried to smile. She looked as if she was focusing very hard, actively not crying.

'Sure.'

'Thanks.' Abigail squeezed her arm, and looked at the unlit roll-up. 'It's really your last ever?'

Joanna looked down at the roll-up too, at the last purple kiss. 'Are you really going to tell him to leave his ex?'

Abigail nodded.

'Then it's really the last ever.'

Abigail hugged her. Abigail was good at hugs, unlike Joanna, who was pretty sure she hugged like she'd read about it some-where. She peeled Abigail off. 'Come on, you're seeing me this evening.'

'Why'd you rather I just walked off? Why do you hate saying goodbye?'

'Is that your bus?' She nodded towards the centre of the traffic jam.

Abigail ran, stilettos clacking on the drying pavements. God, if only this was the last cigarette. She wished it could be, wished she could believe.

The clouds were finally losing out to the sun. Maybe that was why her face felt warm. Or maybe it was the energy of wanting to murder the evening-suited, stick-waving tosser who would no doubt keep Abigail standing outside the stage door until his orchestra's tea break. God, she ached to be useful. But all she could do was give up her own addiction in the daft hope that Abigail really would keep her promise to give up hers in return.

A movement across the road, registering blue. The hand was back. The girl who wasn't Mary brightened at having her attention again. The hand hadn't meant 'stop'. It was reaching. Joanna slid her free hand through her electric blue hair, and the girl who wasn't Mary jumped up and down, waving her hand, her limp brown hair leaping and falling on her stooped shoulders.

But the charity shop door opened and the man with the carrier bags looked a brief little apology towards Joanna; not the usual scared embarrassment of a normal adult faced with blue hair, platforms and thick eye-liner on someone who'd clearly not seen eighteen in a while. It was an apology for the girl's strange behaviour. Was she was disabled in some way? Joanna's boot kicked Café Sanctuary's wall again.

The girl waved harder as they turned towards the corner, leading off Richmond High Street towards St Margaret's. Joanna stalked around Café Sanctuary, on to the cobbled alleyway that ran beside the graveyard. Her last cigarette didn't need to be in front of a church. Even if it was an ex-church.

She rested a metallic toe-cap on the street sign of Duck Alley, smiling her silent 'hello' to the generations of smokers who'd ducked out of Café Sanctuary when it was still St David's to do exactly what she was doing now. The passage was empty. The millionaires' row of former almshouses ran down to an arch that opened on to the French café and the back entrance of the supermarket.

It was dark in the alley. A light from a tiny stained-glass window by Sanctuary's fire escape lit up a maroon coat of arms she'd not noticed before. It was divided into three, with three lions on each section, black on maroon. She traced the black iron letters of 'Vincit Omnia Veritas' with her finger. Truth Conquers All. She could almost taste the coffee she used to sneak into the school library at lunchtime, the only place you learned what you wanted to. Which, being mainly sex and Latin, had been considered equally irrelevant in her school. It had been worth it, the occasional detentions. She'd learnt enough to argue her way out of Dad's church and run off to the theatre. As a set designer, she built her own temples.

The deeper colours of the shield blazed amber as the security light came on above her head. She leaned to one side, then the other, so that dark and bright fought and sparkled over the bodies of the lions.

Had there been someone's reflection in the glass?

She'd go home, soon, after the cigarette.

The last cigarette. Jesus. There was only so long she could put it off. Time to officially become an ex-smoker. She fished for the lighter, which had slipped through the lining yet again. It wasn't about the nicotine. It was the one ritual that was hers. The flame, the cold, the air. The space it created to think. Why was she making herself do this? How was giving up smoking going to make Abigail dump that serial-dumping arsehole? Stupid, stupid idea.

God, her lungs felt so fucking normal. She wanted her body to feel panicked, to know in her bloodstream that this was it: the last rush of delicious emptiness, the last comforting heaviness in the chest. This was the beginning of starvation. Even if her lungs didn't know. Even if her lungs were still having a perfectly good day.

Nothing. Normal cigarette break. Did that mean she wasn't going to do it? Did her body know something she didn't know? That she wasn't going to give up?

Well, she'd show it then. This was it. The panic was setting in now, an open window on a freezing day, cold breeze cutting through a snug room. The chance and the terror of real possibility, real freedom. She raised the lighter and flicked.

'Stop!'

It was her own voice; she'd shouted before she knew she'd shouted.

Wide fingers pressed her hip. Someone's hand was in her pocket. Why had she stopped shouting? Why wasn't she fighting back? He was behind her, tight to her body. She began another shout but felt a mouthful of fist. She tried to bite. Oh shit, he wasn't going to –

Something sliced between her and the body pressed to her back, dragging the fist from her mouth. Her palms slapped the flat of the stained-glass shield. She launched herself back off the window, spinning around to face the scuffle.

If God was telling her He didn't want her to smoke, He'd picked the most ungodly pair of angels in the world. The podgy one, with shoulder-length hair that made his limbs seem too small, looked like a creature evolved from a haystack. Pushing him to the old church wall with a firm thud and a big smile was a tall man in tailored grey. He was built like a stick insect, trying to cover it with a suit that yelled of excess money, and gelled hair that yelled of excess time. Suit had Haystack pinned to the wall now, and was looking over his shoulder at Joanna the same smug way her cat did when triumphing over a very small spider.

'What the fuck do you think you're doing?' she shouted at both of them.

Suit turned from her to his prey, the look smugger than ever.

'I said, what the fuck do you think you're doing?'

Suit looked at her again, his arched eyebrow raising another inch. Joanna had never known hate at first sight until now.

'Well?'

'Well,' murmured Suit, tightening his hold. 'It did look as if you might require . . . '

He was smiling to put her at her ease. To make her feel better about being rescued. The wanker.

'As if I might need what?'

She had to hold his gaze, get back ownership of her situation, her territory. Or Café Sanctuary wouldn't be hers any more. It would be taken over by this memory, be the place she got mugged and humiliated. No way. She was going to show Suit she wasn't shaking with fear, but with fury.

'He looked at me first, you see, but he picked you,' Suit continued.

'I see.' At the edge of her vision and the end of Suit's arm, Haystack's head jerked as the tiny eyes in the wide face darted from her to Suit and back again. He wasn't just overweight, there was a distortion in the shape. Medication? She almost felt sorry for how little chance he had against them. Almost.

'Now, look here, are you going to call the police?'

Look here? Did people really still say look here? Even in Kensington this man would be a tosser. Joanna stuck her tongue in her cheek, rolled it around. 'Didn't see which of you started it.'

'I beg your pardon?' Suit's consonants were getting crisper.

'Two guys fighting. How do I know which of you mugged me?'

'Because it's my jacket in the puddle.'

Joanna looked at the cobbles. Beside the mud and the spilt contents of her broken tobacco tin, a dark grey suit-jacket lay half in and half out of a puddle. The darkness of the water was already soaking up the arms and back. 'What sort of man takes his jacket off before saving a woman from a fucking mugger?'

Suit's expression hovered between furious and fascinated. His eyes were less sharp, the question was being forced inwards. He was doubting himself. Which meant she'd got him. She'd won.

Haystack moved. He must have felt Suit's grip loosen. He looked down the alley, up it. She took a step towards them. Her eyes locked Haystack's. She placed a fingertip on the top of the messy hair and pushed gently, forcing Haystack to look across the damp cobbles to the muddied roll-up. 'That was my last cigarette,' she said. Her voice was shaking. With any luck it sounded like anger.

Haystack made a noise between a grunt and a squeak.

'Disgusting habit,' said Suit.

She stepped back, for a full look at Haystack. 'I was giving up.' She made herself smile, forcing the fear to stay down, safe in her legs. They couldn't wobble – not yet. She had to finish this first.

She drew her arm back.

The punch was quick, beautifully simple, and direct. A single drop of red arced through the air from Haystack's nose towards the puddle with the jacket.

Suit dodged just enough as Haystack's head rolled to the side and forward again. Haystack was aware enough to stare, afraid enough to wait wide-eyed for whatever the mad Goth in front of him would do next. She brought her face in, the right distance for a head-butt. 'Run along,' she whispered.

Haystack skidded sharply at the end of the alley. She waited, listening to the last thuds down the empty high street before the sound was out of range. Then she turned to Suit, trying to match his first patronising smile. The fear must stay in her legs. It would stay in her legs. He mustn't see it in her face, mustn't hear it in her voice. Sanctuary was her place and no one would see she'd been afraid.

'Hope the blood didn't reach your jacket?' she asked.

'Quite.' There was a crotchety sound to Suit's voice now. 'I'm late as it is. That'll teach me to . . . ' He shook his head, raising both palms in a gesture that could mean 'I surrender' or 'fuck off'. But this time she wasn't going to be stopped by any hand.

'Blood washes out. Faster than mud, I expect.'

Suit was searching for words he didn't know, a parting shot he didn't have. 'Ships in the night,' he snapped, grabbing his jacket from the puddle in a passing swoop.

'Ships in the night.' She stood politely to the side for him to drip down the lane towards whichever millionaire's almshouse he called home.

But Suit didn't go up Duck Alley to the cottages. He stepped over her soggy cigarette and unlocked Sanctuary's back door, right beside the stained-glass window with the maroon shield. The door clunked shut behind him, leaving her alone and taking all the strength in her legs with it. She swayed towards the door. Her space, her smoking wall. She leaned her back against the wall, her stinging palms flat to the cool of the glass. But it wasn't strong enough to sustain her now. She slid down to the cobbles.

She knew now why he'd been wearing a suit.

On the other side of Sanctuary's back door, a voice that sounded like Laurence but far snappier was saying 'Ladies and gentlemen, the late Gabriel Openshaw . . . '

There was no answer, just the squeal of a piano stool dragged off its spot and the opening bars of a strangely jazzy version of *Seek Thee First*.

She reached a shaking hand to the cobbles and prised the remains of her roll-up from the mud. She looked at her handiwork, her signature lipstick. She slid the thing into her coat pocket, leant her forehead against the door and closed her eyes, as if listening hard enough would mean she could hide inside the hymn. So much for defending Sanctuary. So much for ships in the night.

Mark Hudson
The Cold Earth

December 409. Northern Gaul

A sharp foot kicked into Nehtan's ribs. Little Vitalis didn't speak but his head jerked up and a quiff of dark hair fell over his face. They were coming out of a wood, huddled together under a thick rug at the back of the Roman army baggage cart. Nehtan rolled her eyes at Vitalis. Was it a game, or was he reminding her that she was his father's slave?

The warmth of the rug and the noise of the cart trundling along the road had lulled her to sleep. She liked being in the cart, with no duties until nightfall, day-dreaming and watching the overgrown countryside pass by. The fields were strangled by weeds and most of the huts had collapsed roofs. It didn't matter, it was only Gaul and they would soon be in another army camp.

She rubbed her ribs and looked at freckle-faced Vitalis. He was clutching his throat and grunting fake coughs as he lifted an imaginary pot of water to his lips. That would mean climbing over the high wooden rails, jumping down and going forwards to find the water-cart, which wouldn't stop for her. The oxen were bad-tempered brutes whose hooves could easily crush a foot.

'Tell you what, let's roll the dice for it. You beat me, and I go for the water. You don't, and we wait until the next stop.'

'I could make you go. I should.'

'You want the soldiers to see that you need a girl to get your water?'

'Eheu! You've got an answer for everything. Where's the dice?'

They rolled and Nehtan won. She looked up to the branches leaning out over them so that her smile of triumph wouldn't provoke Vitalis.

The boy's mouth opened wide as Nehtan heard a loud noise like a flock of raucous crows. She raised herself and froze. Shrieking riders were rushing at the column of Roman soldiers marching in front. For an instant she was jerked back to when wild slave-raiders had grabbed her and her brother all those years ago.

Vitalis shouted at the cart-driver, but the man paid no attention; instead he jumped down, leapt across the ditch and ran away through the scrub. The four soldiers at the back and the drivers of the other carts fled, and Nehtan was left alone with Vitalis. Her mouth was dry and her stomach clenched. She put her hand out to Vitalis. She felt as if she was his mother, not his slave-sister. She stood up again and saw long-haired men on horseback with lances and flashing swords, surrounding the soldiers.

'Holy Mother of God, save us.'

The Romans were silent except for shouted orders. She recognised the voice of Victoricus. The raw screaming of the attackers was overwhelming.

She told Vitalis to get down and was overtaken by a spasm of violent shaking as they clambered off their cart. It was the last in a line of six. Should they follow the cart-drivers? Their Gaulish driver was horrible: twice he had grabbed her breasts and once he had tried to force her into the bushes. In any case, Victoricus was commanding the soldiers. He had always protected her. She allowed Vitalis to pull her by the hand up the line of carts and oxen, towards the roar of clashing iron.

A confused mass of men were fighting in small groups. They looked grim and distant, utterly intent on what they were doing. Bloodied bodies lay on the ground, clutching at wounds in agony or staring with their mouths open. The Romans stood out in their red cloaks and oval shields – some fought with heavy spears and others with long spatha swords. The attackers were barbarian horsemen, wearing bright cloaks.

The noise became louder. She heard a rider's sword come crashing down on a Roman soldier's shield, shattering the rim and cutting through to the chest of the soldier, saw the man stumble backwards. Another barbarian, wild-haired and on foot, tried to get at the soldier, coming in front of the horseman. The Roman desperately thrust his sword at the short man, who parried the blow. The soldier then pushed forwards with his broken shield. Nehtan saw panic on the stocky barbarian's face as his sword caught in the underside of the Roman shield. The Roman lunged forwards for the kill, but a horseman with a conical helmet and a green patchwork tunic skewered the soldier's neck from behind with a lance. A fountain of red shot across the side of the horse.

It couldn't be happening. Nehtan stood still. A horseman glanced at her and she came alive, turning to flee with Vitalis, but he wasn't there. She rushed back down the line of the carts, shouting for him. A woman and an old man, passengers from another cart, were in the way. She pushed past and the old man fell to the ground. She raced down the side of the carts, looking right and left. Vitalis was at the end, pulling something out of the baggage.

'What are you doing? What's this?'

Vitalis was clutching a long kitchen knife. It looked too large in his small hand. He was shaking and his teeth were clenched hard.

She grasped him by his slight shoulders. 'Let go,' he shouted. 'I'm going to help Father.'

A slice of fear shot through Nehtan. Her hands dropped and

Vitalis ran back towards the savage noise. She caught him when he stopped at the last of the carts, and pinioned his arms, making him drop the knife.

'Stop this, we've got to get away.'

'You're a barbarian – like them. Let me fight. Let me go!'

Vitalis struggled in her grip. She saw two of the attackers starting to run towards them. Nehtan grabbed the boy's arm and yanked him back, along the side of the cart. The men were close behind, whooping and swinging their swords high. She ran with Vitalis around a small cart that was being jerked upwards by a panicked, muscular horse. It reared high above them and they ducked under its hooves. The nearest man chasing them screamed as the horse toppled on to him, cracking his bones. The other barbarian stopped to free his comrade. Vitalis ran ahead as Nehtan glanced back. Another long-haired man was racing after them with his sword aimed at her head. She sprinted forward, shouting at Vitalis to run into the woods.

The swordsman was too close. She threw herself to the ground, twisting into a ball, hoping to trip the barbarian up. He fell over her at full tilt and sprawled into the ditch. She leapt up and kicked at the man's hand as he reached for her foot. While the man scrambled for his sword, she ran alongside the last of the carts. Vitalis was jumping across the ditch into the woods.

A barbarian appeared from the other side of the cart, laughing hysterically, circling the air with his sword. Nehtan turned but she was too slow. Out of the corner of her eye she saw the blade come slicing down towards her head. Then – nothing.

*

She sat up on the cold ground and tried to remember what had happened. She was in a ditch on the side of a straggly wood of larch and alder. Above her, a muddy road ran straight as an arrow through grey trees. She felt a pulsating stab in her head. Where was Vitalis?

The light was failing, but she could see her hand was covered with blood and earth. She groaned and felt that her brown cape was wet. She was thirsty. At the bottom of the ditch she made out a trickle of water. She bent forward and drank, cautiously at first and then more fully. She wobbled to her feet, squelching her short hand into the muddy top of the ditch to keep her balance. A wooden cart was on its side and next to it two legs of a horse stuck up, the forelegs hanging down from the knees. Further off, dark shapes stained the road.

Lord God, they're bodies. Holy Jesus. Vitalis? He must have got away . . .

She wanted to shout for the boy, but was it safe? Her muscles were numb and a cold wind bit through her blood-stained clothes. The throbbing in her head made her eyesight ripple disturbingly, like a storm-swept sea surface. She had to get out of the ditch. She hobbled some yards along the stony rut at the bottom of the trench. The effort of stepping out of the slippery hole would be too much, so she knelt and crawled up. Sharp stones penetrated her tunic and cut her knees. Where was he? She stood and stared at round-headed helmets and bits of clothing strewn across the road.

The side of her head throbbed as if it was being gripped by a vice. Thank the Lord it had only been a glancing blow. With her hand she felt her hair, matted with blood. The wound stung badly but her skull was intact. The others hadn't been so lucky: bodies cut open, misshapen faces covered in crimson.

She must breathe. Breathe slowly. Let Vitalis be alive. Lord, let it be all right. If you have taken his father, then leave Vitalis. I pray you, please, let him be.

Only the sounds of chirping birds. She walked towards slumped shapes on the road. The army carts had gone, except a small one on its side. A dead horse lay with its legs splayed and white froth curdled on its lips.

'Is anyone here? Vitalis? Where are you?'

Silence. In Bononia she had heard soldiers talking about Vandal and Alan barbarians rampaging through towns on the eastern side of Gaul. They weren't meant to be here.

With a shock she realised that all of the bodies were Roman. The soldiers' short haircuts and shaven faces made them instantly distinguishable from the long-haired and straggly-bearded barbarians. The barbarian attackers must have taken away their dead and wounded in the carts. Some of the dead had been stripped of their capes and many had lost their tough boots. In front of her, a spillage of congealed red coloured the white chest of a half-naked man. Heavy legionary spears lay on the ground. The dead men were slumped in awkward positions, with their heads thrown back or with an arm bent under their side, as if they had been tossed aside by a giant. Several had Roman darts sticking into them. The attackers seemed to have finished off the wounded. The Romans would have done the same if they had won, though they wouldn't have left any weapons behind.

Nehtan looked all around her. Vitalis must be hiding somewhere else; he had run the other way. The small fields behind the soldiers were desolate and had not been cultivated. Twilight deepened as she went back to the place where the road came out of the wood. After a minute she stumbled against something. My God, a dead body! But it was a big sack, half full of cabbages. She was overcome by exhaustion and started to cry.

'Lord God, don't do this to me. Let it not be your will. Let me die later, as long as I find him alive.'

She went back to the upturned cart and slumped down against it. It was too dark to see much and the cold was biting. She had an idea and fetched the cabbage sack, dumping the vegetables on the ground. She got into the sack and huddled down, trying to close the top of the sack over her. It would have to do. She closed her eyes and saw swords cutting through red-cloaked flesh, metal flashing into jellied faces. Vitalis? Maybe he had run away and found a village. He would be crying for her and his father, but her search would have to wait until dawn.

*

She awoke to a pale light, cold, wet, and with a terrible thirst that she thrust aside. She was not going to die in this miserable place. With a shock she realised that she was free, she could escape her slave-life and find her family. But how? They were lifetimes away, across the sea, in the far north of Britannia. Freedom meant nothing without Vitalis, without knowing he was all right. What should she do? As a slave she always had a purpose. Now, there was no one to ask. Lying inside the sack, holding her head with both hands, she reached back for a sense of calmness. The services, that quiet place she found. Silently she said a prayer.

> May grace come
> and may this world pass away.
> Hosanna to the God of David.
> If anyone is holy,
> let him come;
> if anyone is not,
> let him repent.
> Maranatha. Amen.

She repeated it over and over, begging the Lord to help her, for strength, not a miracle. She did not dare to look outside the sack. There might be people watching – about to rip the sack open and grab her. She waited and listened for the breathing of others. Nothing. She forced herself to peep out into the daylight. It was early and the sun was low. There was no one in sight, at least, no one alive. Crows and magpies were cackling loudly and pecking at bodies. Further off, foxes were ripping flesh, fighting over slithery innards. Nehtan screamed at them as she stumbled out of the sack. The birds looked up and the nearest flew off. The foxes ignored her. She shouted again and turned in the direction of Bononia, where they had come from. The coastal city was three days' cart-ride away.

She must find Vitalis. She walked numbly down the road, with her arms crossed and shivering. The wood on either side was thin and scruffy, dotted with mossy outcrops and large clumps of brambles. A stab of hunger shot up from her belly. The cabbages she had chucked out of the sack? But she did not want to return to the animals tearing at raw bodies. She spotted a puddle between two rowans and jumped across the ditch to scoop up some water. It tasted brackish, like stale beer.

She didn't want to look for Victoricus. If he were alive, he would have come to find her, and if he was dead, she couldn't bear the thought of his hacked body. But she would find his son. She forced herself to walk down the road through the wood into which Vitalis had fled. Her long hair was heavy with blood and mud. The sun was warm and her head was hot. She wished she had been braver and had gone back to grab some of the cabbages. The white tops of mushrooms glistened on the edge of the road. Victoricus would have known which ones were safe. She longed for someone to talk to.

She heard a loud screech from the trees ahead, froze and held her breath. It wasn't Vitalis. Was it a bird, frightened by someone hiding in the thicket? Or a spirit, a dead soldier's spirit, angry at not being buried? She reached for the amulet hanging around her neck and rubbed the incised cross three times with her thumb.

Christ Jesus, let it not be a spirit. Send it away.

There was another screech and a crow flew towards her. She shrieked and ran back down the road. When she stopped running, she turned and decided to make a loop across the bare land on the other side of the road, to avoid the thicket from where the crow came. She struggled across the boggy ground and shouted for Vitalis.

What to do? Damn him! She crossed herself. If Vitalis hadn't run away she wouldn't be alone. She sat down on the muddy grass and hugged her shoulders. A sparrow flitted by. Was it a sign? If she wanted to get back to her village above the Wall, she'd have to be brave. She stood up and shouted towards the thicket.

'I'm coming, I'm coming, whoever you are. Don't be a spirit!'

What was she saying? She was a Christian. The Lord would protect her. She clutched her amulet and trudged across puddles to reach the thicket. It was shadowed, with undergrowth and hawthorn bushes beneath a canopy of angled alder.

'Vitalis!'

She picked her way in. Brambles tore her leg so she used a stick to bash the thorny stems back. The exertion made her head sear with pain, as if someone was slowly peeling the skin off her scalp. Then, in amongst the decaying greenery, she saw a shape, a small body in a familiar bluish tunic. No!

It was Vitalis. Maybe he was asleep? He lay face down and his back was bloody. She sobbed and knelt, stroking the dark brown hair and the freckled cheek. He was five years younger than her. She hesitated before she turned him over. Thank God, his eyes were shut. His cheekbones were tight, crushed, and his chin looked wrong. She cradled his head, held him and cried softly.

'Oh, Lord God, why does this have to be?'

Who had killed him, this far away from the carts? She looked around: was the killer watching her? She held her breath. After a while, she lay Vitalis back down. If someone was there, they would have attacked her already . . . surely? Vitalis's body looked empty and dumped out, like the sack she had slept in.

She lay on her side, facing away from him. Her belly gripped painfully. Vitalis had been teasing her only yesterday . . . Better not to think, better to listen to the blackbirds and thrushes. Their twitter was just like any other day, but it wasn't any other day, it was horribly different and raw. At church, they had sung about the branches of the one tree, all given life for Christ, all creation part of him. But did Vitalis's death have to be part of it? Her eyes closed and a cold oblivion settled over her.

Sarah Park
Skin

I wasn't supposed to be here. Skyscrapers reflected the sun's rays into the square, their facades rippling like vertical pools of black water. It was hot and airless and men in pinstriped trousers huddled under doorways for shelter. They talked on phones and paced in slivers of shade, occasionally looking up and shielding their eyes as though holding private conversations with the sun.

Only two hours ago, I was sitting on a sofa in Rachael's white kitchen receiving a long list of instructions about how to look after her son and where we would spend our first time alone together. The orders were peppered with the noise of expensive kitchen appliances and her voice rose and fell as she talked.

'I've checked the weather and it'll be fine all day, so a walk is perfect, a short walk, not too long, we don't want him getting too hot.' Her giggle had no heart and she busied herself with washing the breakfast dishes. 'He's so sweet,' she said, rubbing the counter top furiously at a mark I couldn't see. 'He seems to like looking at the birds, so I recommend a park. Not Hyde Park though, not a park full of weirdos. And not too far away. Just a nice park. Richmond. Richmond's nice.' She looked up and smiled a sad smile. 'I'm sorry, I just worry. He's my little boy.'

I went over and put my arms around her. Her body went slack. I pulled back her hair and looked at her face; she was wearing pale pink lipstick. 'I know you are worried but you need to get this meeting out of the way and I am here to help you do that. You know you can trust me to look after him.'

Thomas was six months old. Rachael and Michael had given him his grandfather's name, on his dad's side. 'It was really important to him,' Rachael had whispered. It wasn't that she didn't like the name, but we often held circular conversations on how we could prevent Thomas ever becoming Tommy or Tommo merely due to people's fondness for slicing off the letters of a perfectly good name and adding their own. 'I don't know why people want to be so familiar all the time,' said Rachael. 'Though, look at K Mids. She became Catherine. I've not heard her once be called Kate since she married Wills.'

'I think it's called royal protocol.'

'But I'm not a royal and I call her Catherine.'

The only person who called him Tommy was me and when she wasn't listening I spoke the name softly in his ear. Tommy. I am his godmother and today he was going to be all mine.

The square was only a twenty-minute taxi ride from Richmond Park and Tommy had fallen asleep in his blue cocoon as soon as his mother had tucked him in. Leaning down under the shade of soft material, I mimicked her actions and with the tips of my fingers pressed the white sheet into his chest and around his neck. He didn't move except for a tiny jerk of his fist and a barely audible gasp.

His skin was the colour of milk, too creamy for the coldness of chalk, too soft to be porcelain; even in scrutiny there was not the trace of a blemish. Its purity mesmerised me, probably because my own skin was a canvas of imperfection that started in infancy and continued through adulthood; my face burnt in an accident in childhood; as a junior my cheeks flared with rosacea under the hot glare of the school yard; and as boys became objects to peek at quickly over class textbooks, a cruel acne made me withdraw with the same rapidity.

I wanted to protect it. 'Don't you worry,' I whispered. 'I'll give you all the skin advice you need when you grow up. No sun for you. Or sweets.' I blew gently into the hood, re-tucking him in once more. 'You're not too hot, are you?'

We were standing by the restaurant that had brought me here, an expensive chain of bland, Italian food. The porch was bare except for seven lonely coat-hangers shaped like deer antlers. I could hear the tinny clatter of plates among the murmur of male voices, a lunchtime of rich mushroom sauce and red wine spilling over into late afternoon. 'Wish me luck, Tommy,' I whispered into the hooded milky smell. The pinstripes were still milling outside. It wasn't too late to turn back but I'd thought about this too often. I carefully positioned the buggy where it was visible through the window and pushed open the door. A pale-skinned man of about twenty was replacing glasses behind the bar.

'Hi, does Nick work here?'

'Yeah, he's in the back.' He paused and smiled. 'Who shall I say it is?'

I hadn't thought of having to announce myself, creating an opportunity for him to say he was busy. I gave him what I hoped was my most charming smile. 'Tell him it's a surprise . . . but a good one.'

He smirked and walked away, throwing a cloth over his shoulder. I turned round and looked at the buggy and tried to replace the images in my head of a sleeping child. My mind was imagining what I was about to see: the bright blue eyes, the short, shaven hair, the wide, assured smile; slightly teasing, always playful. I needed to sober the thoughts in my head, to rid them of their giddiness, but I was intoxicated by the memories from back when Nick and I were together, before he made me cry so many times.

I heard him before I saw him, a distant echo. 'Wow! Laura!' He hesitated then fixed his composure with a big smile and stepped towards me in the purposeful, gangling stride that used to scoop me up and lead me by the hand to wherever we wanted to go.

'Hello, Nick. Surprised?'

'Gosh, Jesus . . . yes, I am surprised. How did you know I was still here? But a lovely surprise. How are you?' It was clear he hadn't expected to see me again.

'I thought I would pop in on the off-chance . . . I wanted to catch up.'

He waited for me to say more.

'I hope this isn't a bad time . . . if you're busy . . . ' I looked around the restaurant floor. There were eight, maybe ten grey heads bobbing and nodding at tables. It was quiet. I knew he had just finished his shift, for the past six Fridays I had watched him leave the restaurant at this time.

'No, no, look,' he said raising his arm towards the heads. 'Dead. So, as always, I am at your service.' He curled one arm behind his back and bowed courteously. He was teasing me like he used to. I felt my churning stomach relax and flip at the same time. He hadn't changed at all.

*

I had looked at that very same spot on the top of his head fifteen months ago when, sitting on the edge of my bed, he had bent down to tie his shoelaces. He had been getting ready to leave and while he searched for his keys and checked his phone my brain had sped through what I could do to stop him, the moment when he'd give me a peck on the cheek ('See you!' 'Not if I see you first, ha ha!'). And in the silence and seconds that slipped passed I had watched for the tiniest sign that he was slowing down, trying to hold the moment for as long as he could so that one of us could say something. Instead his other foot had brushed the carpet as it came forward and his fingers spun the lace, once, twice, then round itself, pulling it into a double knot.

*

Nick snapped upright, clapped his hands and turned to his colleague who was hovering and drying the inside of the same glass, half-listening. 'Wine, we must have wine,' and he reached out a hand to me. 'You will stay for one, won't you . . . we have a lovely Picpoul, very fresh, very crisp?' His manner was charged and he scampered back and forth pointing at bottles, clasping his hands and rubbing them together. He chatted to the air around him and his words floated in and out. I glanced round to check I could still see the buggy outside.

'Never busy on a Friday . . . bankers at their holiday homes. Lucky you caught me . . . just finished. Otherwise stuck with this jackass.' He nodded towards the bar and there was deep male laughter. Young girls in black and white walked past and looked straight at me before staking their territory. 'You not gone yet, Nick? I want to go out for a fag. Pete, say something that will make him eff off.'

Nick laughed with them but he was preoccupied.

'So, gosh, this is a surprise. You look well,' he said.

I looked down at my outfit, a black, lightweight, A-line dress, patent black pumps, a safe outfit. 'Well, I'm not so sure, not at the moment anyway.' He looked quizzical.

'You always looked good, you know that,' he said.

I pulled a face. 'Things were different then. And I'll just have a sparkling water.'

'Blimey, you've changed since the last time I saw you, when was that by the way?' He cocked his head towards the ceiling, one hand holding a fragile-looking glass by its stem, his actions exaggerated like pantomime. 'It must be, what, a year, two? Tell me it can't be two.'

'Fifteen months.' I said.

'Wow, precise.' His words mocked but I remained silent and took my eyes off him, conscious that I was staring. Towards the end he used to snap, 'Stop staring at me!' He just didn't seem to understand how beautiful I thought he was.

'Do you wanna grab a seat, perhaps over there?' He pointed to a small round table for two at the edge of the dining space and glanced at his watch. 'Definitely have time for a quick one.'

The table had two high metal stools that screeched on the tiles as I pulled and pushed them away. I slid on to the one facing the door so I could see the buggy. I hated high stools, they weren't designed for women. Hiking up my skirt, I clambered on to the rung and wondered what to do with my handbag. It was too big for the table. I placed it on my knee but felt matronly. I bent down and lowered it to the floor, my head practically underneath the table.

'You all right down there?' The stool opposite me screeched again and Nick placed glasses of wine and water on the table, sliding his slender body easily on to the chair. I noticed they were small measures of liquid in large glasses. 'The stools, they're too high,' I said. I was pleased when he laughed.

'So you're still running this place, are you?' I asked. He took a slug of wine and nodded, swallowing. 'Yeah, it's good for now. The pay is good; team's great. The group who own it have loads of restaurants over the country and especially in London.' I smiled and let him talk and nodded to show him I understood, I wanted to anchor him to how he felt when we used to spend whole evenings talking and when he said, 'You really listen to me, don't you? I think you're the only person who does and I love it,' before kissing me on the nose and pulling me closer. I leant my head to the side and smiled softly, my eyes meeting his. He stopped talking and we were both silent. We looked at each other and his blue eyes were calm. It was time.

'Nick. There's a reason why I've come here today. I want you to meet a little someone.' I slipped off the stool, picked up my handbag and walked towards the door. I heard an abrupt screech and knew he'd turned round. I walked slowly, taking considered steps and imagining what he would be seeing. My back, slender, composed, my blonde hair, bright and soft against black material, the brightness outside, and to the far left edge of the porch, a child's buggy. He hadn't moved by the time I opened the door and when I turned to look at the sleeping baby I saw him staring. As if someone suddenly barked an order at him from the shadows, he launched off his stool and came towards me in one movement. He swung open the door and looked from me to the buggy.

'So, who is this?'

I said nothing.

'What, you've had a baby? What, it's yours or . . .?' He was bemused and irritated and his eyes darted from me to the buggy and back again. He waited for me to say something. I could see his colleague behind the bar still drying glasses; it was probably the same glass.

'We've had a baby, Nick.'

His silence was broken with a snorting noise. 'What the fuck do you mean, we've had a baby . . . how have we had a baby?'

I didn't answer as I leant into the warm, milky hood. Supporting his head, I lifted the sleeping bundle out of the pram and made a 'shhhhh' noise into his ear.

'Are you fucking kidding me, is this a joke?' The light that danced in his eyes had gone out and he looked at me, horrified, and then sank against the glass door. He'd placed his hands on his thighs and bowed his head as though recovering from an early morning sprint. He looked up at me. 'How old is he, what the fuck do you mean he's mine?'

'He's six months old. I gave birth to him on the ninth of February.' I was surprised by how calm my voice sounded.

'Just wait one minute. Slow the fuck down. How is this possible? I would have known, why is this happening now?'

I had anticipated this. It would have been too much to ask for him to take his baby in his arms straight away. I knew it would be a shock and that the best thing for him would be to come to his own understanding. I kept silent and stared at him while gently rocking little Tom. Nick's face moulded into strange shapes with each new emotion as he made rapid, fag-packet calculations of times and dates.

'That night.' He laughed abruptly. 'When we went to that pub, near where you live and I came back to yours.'

I nodded.

'But I thought you were on the pill.'

I slowly rocked the bundle from side to side. 'I was. I couldn't believe it either when I found out. The doctors said that it is rare but it happens. I suppose you could say we were unlucky, but I can't. Look at him. I feel very lucky.'

For the first time since I had cradled the baby, Nick looked at him. He was a child himself, frightened and inexperienced. He took a step towards us.

'Nick, meet Tommy.'

Nick didn't touch him or say anything, and we stood together, the three of us, in a silence broken only by the low vibration of a phone ringing in my handbag.

Natalia Bulgakova
WAR

In one day the city had become unrecognisable, flooded by human smells, filled with a growing roar, white with the dust from thousands and thousands of marching troops.

From the surrounding provinces and remote corners of the vast empire endless trains full of reservists were arriving in colourful, eclectic attire. They were camped all over the town waiting to change into army uniform and be sent off to the front. The sale of alcohol had been prohibited from the first day of the war, and they were whiling away the time gathered around small fires drinking tea, playing cards and telling endless stories.

Bruce did not remember falling asleep at his desk or crawling to the sofa. He was roused at six in the morning by the marching troops outside. The sun was already up, and walking home in the pleasant coolness of an early hour, he could smell burning wood from the small fires and watched soldiers busy with boiling watery soup and tea in their small tin kettles.

Jean was in bed. He kissed her on the forehead. She smiled in her sleep and murmured, 'It is in the box. In the blue box.' He changed his shirt and went back to the Consulate.

*

In a few hours, telegrams started arriving. Some were addressed to the Consul-General, some to the Ambassador, a few to Lord Grey, a dozen to the King and about as many to Bruce himself. They all wanted to know, 'What is England doing? Why has she not yet declared war . . .? If she had declared war on Germany at once there would have been no war at all . . . ' The telegrams were soon followed by letters and calls threatening, pleading and grumbling about Britain not joining the Allies. Leaving the office late at night, Bruce had to take the back exit to avoid a small demonstration demanding that England take urgent action. The demonstration grew daily, and by the morning of Wednesday, 5th August, the crowd was big enough to block his way to the Consulate-General.

Bruce stopped at the corner. He overheard voices calling for the Consul and saw a couple of hats fly towards the windows. He was about to turn back when he remembered that Bayley, who spoke no Russian and had only one working eye to assess the situation, was about to arrive in his private coach, driven by a half-deaf coachman, Ivan. He hesitated. He couldn't leave him now . . . Yet what could he do? Address the crowd in his best Russian? But what could he tell them? Nobody was going to believe him if he said that he had not got the slightest idea what England's next step would be.

Somebody cried out, 'There! He is there! That one with funny ears! Make way for the British Vice-Consul!' A woman in a straw hat rushed towards him, waving a bouquet of blue flowers, and before he could understand what was going on he was lifted up by dozens of hands and passed over the heads of the crowd towards the entrance. Hundreds of thundering voices shouted, 'Long live England!'

Only when his feet touched the ground again did he realise what had happened. Last night Britain had declared war on

Germany. British men had never been so popular on the streets of Moscow.

*

In the afternoon Lyki stopped by the Consulate-General. Wiping away tears of joy, and blowing his nose with an enormous pink handkerchief, he embraced everyone on his way, 'This war will be quick and victorious! And what's more, my dear Lockhart, this won't be a mere military victory. This will be a victory of spirit!'

He turned on his heels and suddenly burst out with laughter, 'Why do the Germans spell *Kultur* with a K?' Bayley, puffing on a favourite cigar, looked at him with suspicion and shrugged his shoulders. Lyki made another turn on the heels, 'Because Great Britain has command of all the seas!'

Together, he and Lyki strolled down the Petrovskii Boulevard to the Hermitage Restaurant to celebrate the Russian–British alliance. The air smelled of baked apples and the first fallen leaves rustled under their feet. Bruce was glad that this summer was almost over. He longed for a breath of fresh autumn air, a feeling of frostbite on his cheeks; he missed the cleanness of the snow.

People in small groups were rushing past them, all deep in conversation, gesticulating, nodding, touching each other's arms. They were talking about the war; now everything was all about the war. Small gatherings on almost every square were peppered with patriotic placards. On the corner with the Kolobovskii lane, three little boys in marine suits were crawling around the lamp-post, trying to dig it out with bare hands and little sticks, forgotten by their nannies who were absorbed in the latest newspaper.

The restaurant was full, but at the magic words 'our ally Britain' Bruce and Lyki were immediately taken to the best table by the window, half-hidden behind the row of fig trees. Soon they were joined by the war correspondent McCullagh and Stephen Graham of *The Times* who was in Moscow on his way to Petrograd from the Altai Mountains, where he had been writing reports on the Far East.

The four men sat around the table laid with *zakuski* of pickles, meat cuts and herring, toasting one another with delicate porcelain cups. Since the prohibition on alcohol, Moscow restaurants were serving vodka in small samovars and ice-cold teapots, but only for the regulars.

McCullagh was saying he had just arrived from London through St Petersburg on what must have been the last train over the German frontier. He had seen Russian troops lying with guns ready along the banks of the River Wirballen. 'I shared a compartment with a group of dentists coming back from the congress in Brighton. They are all volunteering to go to the front . . . You'd better have your teeth sorted by now. God only know how long this war will drag on . . . '

Lyki waved him away. 'Not long, I assure you! Besides, we were not the ones who started it. We are defending, not attacking; for us this is the war of honour and spirit and brotherhood. The war that, if you wish, will get a few things straight back home too.'

McCullagh looked at the delicate porcelain cup in his rough red fingers and took a sip, 'In Petersburg – sorry, I mean Petrograd – I saw something I will not forget as long as I live. I was walking on Berlinskaya Street – I mean, Londonskaya Street – and was about to turn into the Nevsky Prospect when I heard the strangest noise . . . it was outlandish, a sort of a dying beast's last outcry. I turned around and saw pieces of broken furniture on the pavement on the other side of the street. Then a similar noise again, and something hit the pavement right behind me. "This is not furniture," thought I, "this sounds like a mad giant" and then "boooo-booo-booo," and I honestly thought that I was about to be hit by a falling wall. It is hard to describe. A piano had been thrown from the balcony on the third floor and landed a few metres behind me. You know, German-made pianos, sewing machines, utensils of all sorts are being thrown out into the streets all over the city . . . They are the first casualties . . . '

'This will not last long,' Lyki's face was flaming, 'This war will be the shortest in history. Once it is over . . . '

'But this country is so vast . . . ' sighed Graham, who had been silent until now. 'At the exact time you saw those pianos flying out of the windows in Petrograd, I was about to leave the village of Altai Cossacks on the Chinese frontier. Early in the morning the telegram arrived, just one line, ordering mobilisation. In other words . . . war. You know that the Cossacks are the most loyal of the tsarist troops, they're ready to fight the enemy at any time. Immediately, the commotion starts, the entire day a whirlpool of horses, swords, uniforms. Not a minute wasted. But who was the enemy? Nobody knew and the telegram gave no indication.' He paused and waited for the waiter to replace an empty teapot with a new one, painted with golden polka dots and red flowers. 'So they decided it must be China. Naturally, Russia had pushed too far into Mongolia and China declared war. For a few hours everybody was getting ready to go to war with China. Then a rumour came that the war was with England. Even better . . . ' he smiled. 'So I decided to leave at dusk. And just when I was saying goodbye to a local priest, the truth reached the village. And guess what? They just refused to believe it.' He shook his head. 'But whether they believe or not, these men from the frontier of Mongolia will be going to fight on the plains of Austria and Poland.'

*

Graham said he had to catch a train to Petrograd and Bruce went with him to the station. It was crowded with ensigns and their families. Windows, walls, benches were covered with icons, adorned with flowers and embroidered towels. The long, thin faces of the saints were lit by flickering candles, some mournful, others frantic.

They watched men going to war with their little tin kettles and belongings wrapped up in coloured handkerchiefs. Bearded priests in long black dresses strolled along the platforms with smoking censers, making the sign of the cross over the crowds. Coaches were filled with men, looking out of the windows with amused and inquisitive expressions.

Graham, who in his Russian travel dress resembled a provincial salesman, was generous with his tobacco and was soon surrounded by a small group of peasant soldiers.

'Thank you, brother, God knows when next time we'll be having a decent smoke,' said a small sombre soldier, looking at his boots.

'Sooner than you think!' A smiley redhead looked around for support. 'We'll be smoking best Austrian and German cigarettes before you know.'

Another soldier with chiselled cheekbones and piercing dark eyes slowly scratched his head, 'Why would Germans side with Austria? I met a few Germans in Petersburg. Good business people . . . Reasonable folk.' He put his hat back on and nodded reassuringly, 'We should turn them to our side to fight the foxy Austrians.'

More people joined the circle. Bruce noticed a country doctor who was leaving for the front surrounded by his family. To stop his wife from weeping, he brought them closer to the group, took out a small notebook, and started scribbling down bits of conversation. A tall peasant with oily blond hair joined the circle and, squinting at the doctor's notebook, raised his voice. 'The German Tsar sold his soul to the Devil when he was a young boy!' He made sure the doctor wrote this down, and continued, his blue eyes bulging. 'Now they are both in it to destroy the Orthodox faith! To see us Orthodox folk thrive is a true torture for them, equal to the fire of hell!' Bruce watched the doctor wrote everything down without a trace of emotion on his face.

After Graham found his coach, Bruce waved him goodbye and walked further down the platform. The train made a loud noise, followed by a jolt, and a sudden gasp from thousands of people froze in the air. Another jerk, and a few sobs went through the crowd, voices calling out, 'God be with you! Come home soon!' Finally the train moved, and silence fell, accompanied by hundreds of waving handkerchiefs and brave, tearful smiles.

An old woman, realising that she was still holding her son's travel bag, rushed through the crowd back to the moving train, 'Wait, Nikita, *sinochek*, wait! Your favourites, egg pies, just like you always loved. I was baking all night . . . My boy, my little nightingale!' But she was too late. She did not know where to go and simply sank on to the station floor, clutching the grey bag to her chest, looking around at the flow of people, 'What am I going to do now? *Sinochek moi!*' Bruce's eyes met with hers and a cold shiver ran down his back. He reached into his pocket, but then hesitated and stepped back. She would not take any kopeks from him . . .

Another soldier kneeled next to the woman with a few kind words and helped her to get up. She opened her bag to give him the pies wrapped in a linen towel, but then changed her mind hastily and handed him the whole bag. The soldier accepted with a bow and after she had crossed his forehead, the woman turned around and slowly walked away without looking back. With a strange sense of relief, Bruce left the building.

Outside, the August night was warm and quiet. The bright white Milky Way crossed the sky right above the train station. A shooting star went down in the west, leaving behind a long silver-white tail, in the direction where all the trains were heading. Bruce wondered what those trenches were like. Were they deep? Did they smell of wet soil? He bent down and grabbed a handful of dry fallen leaves. They smelled of home.

Jay Norbury
All's Fair

At one side of the river a troop of cavalry stood, their shields gleaming in the shallow winter sun. The riders seemed to sense the power in their horses' muscled hindquarters, and rode with swords raised, their mouths rounded in an everlasting cry for battle as behind them the green hills rolled. And each horse was not just a horse, but a hundred horses. Each man was not a man, but an entire battalion.

Uncle Alan stood at the big folding table and breathed heavily. He had clattered into my room at six o'clock that morning and spent three hours with a tiny paintbrush in his hand, heaving his bulbous frame over the miniature plastic figures. When they were finished he lined them up on the windowsill to dry, and around the edges of the table he arranged various mounds of paper mâché, over which he laid a green felt cover with a sparkling blue ribbon down the middle. This served as the river. At one end of the battle-field, the ribbon had come away from the fabric and begun to fray.

I sighed under the blanket and waited for him to leave.

'I'll need the room tonight, Ricky,' he said, testing one of the painted figures with his thumb.

'Okay.'

'All night, I mean.'

He ran the flat of his palm over his hair, and from the slick, grey tangle, tiny crumbs of white went tumbling to his shoulders. As he spoke he did not look away from the table.

'Young lad like you should be out of bed by now,' he said. 'Thirteen years old and still in bed at this time.'

Holding a notepad in one hand, he took some archers and some infantrymen from a box on the floor and arranged them in different formations, drawing diagrams of their positions and chewing the stump of a wooden pencil.

'Let's say three o'clock, Ricky,' he said. 'That's plenty of time after we get back from Halifax.'

I pulled the blanket over my head and breathed into the space underneath. There was the rattle of plastic as Uncle Alan upended his bag of dice on to my writing desk, and at the word Halifax a tide of panic began to churn under my ribs.

'Ricky,' Uncle Alan said.

I pulled the blanket down to reveal my face.

'Downstairs by three o'clock.' He nodded slowly, turning the pencil between his teeth. 'And keep your door shut so that bloody dog doesn't get in.'

'Okay.'

As he was leaving he turned towards me with one hand on the doorknob and shook his head: 'Young lad like you.'

I slid out of bed and pulled on the jeans Aunty Lorraine had folded on the cabinet. Looking over the half-empty battlefield I felt the turmoil in my stomach start to wind its way upwards. An idea occurred to me. I put on an extra tee-shirt under my jumper and knelt down with my forehead pressed against the radiator. Then in the mirror I drew my eyebrows into an ashen frown and hunched my shoulders as I went down to breakfast.

*

'You'll be looking forward to a trip to Halifax, Ricky,' Uncle Alan said as Aunty Lorraine stirred his tea. I could hear the low thrum of the dryer in the basement and the moist sound of scrambled egg against the insides of his mouth. The salt smell of bacon hung in my nostrils.

'I said you'll be looking forward to a trip to Halifax.'

I nodded sadly and swayed in my chair. If I tensed the muscles at the back of my throat I could make it feel as if I was about to throw up. Aunty Lorraine put a plate in front of me and held a big cool hand against my head, the gold band on her ring finger hard against my temple.

'Are you feeling all right, love?' she said, and pushed the hexagonal frames of her glasses back along her nose.

I said I didn't know, and looked at the floor. Uncle Alan paused with his knife and fork in his hands, and as he examined me his tongue slid out to capture a speck of egg on his bottom lip.

'He's fine.'

'He feels hot.'

'Well, anybody'd be hot lying in bed all – ' he grimaced and threw back his head, reaching for his leg as if it were caught in something. 'Bloody hell!' he said, 'Can't I even eat my bloody breakfast in peace? Go on, bugger off!'

From under the table came a rough see-sawing of breath as Charlie thumped his tail against Uncle Alan's faded corduroys.

'Begging for scraps, as usual,' he said.

The shin of my jeans warmed as Charlie leant his weight into it, his muzzle tickling my feet with short, humid gasps. I laid my knife and fork beside my plate and peered up at Aunty Lorraine.

'Alan, I'm not sure Ricky's up to it today,' she said, bending down to ruffle the skin behind Charlie's ears. 'He's not eating his breakfast.'

'Enough now, Ricky. Get it down you, lad.' Uncle Alan wiped

his plate with a square of white bread and folded it into his mouth. He emptied his mug and stood up, holding his belt buckle under his gut. 'We're going, and that's that.'

He snorted and left his empty plate on the table.

'And don't go feeding that dog bacon,' he said from the living room, 'or he'll never learn.'

Standing next to my chair, Aunty Lorraine pulled my head into the soft expanse of her midriff. The flesh of her ruddy ankles was reflected in the oven door.

'Go get your coat on, love,' she said, and as I climbed the stairs I heard a wet smack followed by Charlie's paws scrambling across the kitchen.

I took my coat from my wardrobe and picked up a handful of dice from the desk. Some of them had numbers on, and some had faux-metallic lettering which spelled out the names of war manoeuvres, like siege and enfilade. Later, Colin would come over and he and Uncle Alan would throw the dice and make the soldiers fight each other under the big spotlight. A roll of the dice, Uncle Alan had once explained to me, could take you to the brink of victory or complete annihilation. War was not just a game of strategy, you had to understand, but of chance and opportunity as well.

Leaving the door ajar, I dropped the dice behind the radiator and went downstairs.

*

From the twentieth floor you could see all over Halifax. The low-angled morning light skimmed the rooftops but seemed to stop short of the damp, forgotten tower block, which stood at the outer end of the North Bridge. In Sarah's living room there was the hum of a two-bar heater and the bass end of the neighbours' television, and after Aunty Lorraine had made us each a cup of scalding black tea we all sat facing each other on different-sized chairs. In the middle stood a narrow table with chips and cigarette burns along the edges. I blew on my tea and sent puffs of steam disappearing towards the ceiling.

'Yeh, been all right actually. So, yeh . . . been all right . . . '

Sarah trailed off her sentences with a thin, stuttering laugh and used the thumbnail of her cigarette hand to scratch her forehead, dropping flakes of ash in her hair. Uncle Alan had wanted to know how she was getting on, and when she said she was all right actually, it was as if she and everybody else ought to be surprised by the fact. With her free hand she picked at something just inside the cuff of her sweatpants and winced as it came free.

'Well, it looks great, Sarah,' Uncle Alan said, hoisting himself forward in his chair and looking around as if he had just arrived. 'Really great.' He nodded approvingly and raised his eyebrows at Aunty Lorraine, as if this was something he had told her to expect. Then he spoke in a loud voice and asked me about a lot of things he already knew, like how school was and who my friends were, and Sarah would say 'that's nice', or 'that's good then,' and give a silly, startled laugh. She was younger than Aunty Lorraine, but her features seemed somehow thinner and less permanent, like a bad copy in pencil.

'You were looking forward to coming today, weren't you Ricky?' Uncle Alan said.

I nodded at him across the table. Sarah pulled her legs up and hugged her knees, her feet resting on the edge of her seat.

'Wouldn't it be nice if we could do this a bit more regular now, Sarah?' Uncle Alan said. 'You know, now that you're . . . erm . . . '

But Sarah was biting her thumbnail and looking out of the window. She had begun to pump the toes of her tattered slippers up and down, pivoting on the heel. I wondered whether she ever ate anything, or whether she just carried on like that all day, smoking and staring out of the window.

'Wouldn't that be nice, Sarah?'

'Yeh,' said Sarah. 'Yeh, that'd be fine,' and the restless motion of her feet stopped for a moment as she lit another cigarette.

'Well, Alan,' said Aunty Lorraine, one finger on the bridge of her spectacles, 'let's see if we have time in the next few – '

'I bet it's nice for you as well Ricky, isn't it?' Uncle Alan said, before she could finish. He ran his palm along the shiny, matted surface of his hair and seemed to hesitate, leaning forward and smiling with grim intent: 'I bet it's nice to see your mum?'

Sarah clamped a mottled fist across her body to support the elbow of her smoking arm, and the sunken contours of her face disappeared in a spiral of grey.

'It must be nice to see your mum's house, Ricky?'

I said it was nice.

'Aw,' said Sarah, screwing her eyes shut. She reached across from the chair opposite and brushed her yellow fingers along my arm. After a burst of shrill laughter she began to look very serious, cradling her forehead in one hand.

And after that it seemed as if nobody knew what to say. An uncomfortable gloom seemed to gather, and at times Uncle Alan would sit up and look around as if he'd just remembered something, only to sink back in his chair, and Sarah would laugh stupidly and take a drag on her cigarette. Aunty Lorraine pursed her lips and stared at the floor, and after a while she said we ought to get a wriggle on.

As we drove home I closed my eyes and gave myself over to the gentle back-and-forth movement of the car, until I awoke to hear Uncle Alan whispering angrily.

'She's your sister, Lorraine, not mine.'

'Not now, Alan.'

'You should be encouraging her to take responsibility.'

'She's ill, Alan.'

'It's not a disease if you choose to do it. Anyway isn't this new stuff supposed to help her off it? She's too used to living on hand-outs, that's the problem. There's only one medicine for that, Lorraine.'

But he didn't say what it was.

*

'Are you sure you haven't seen them, Ricky? Absolutely sure?'

'He says he's sure, Alan,' said Aunty Lorraine, threading my school trousers through a wire hanger.

'Lorraine,' he said. 'They were there this morning, and now they're not.'

I stared at the TV and shook my head, feeling a traitorous prickle in my cheeks.

I had been sent down to the living room when Colin arrived, and he and Uncle Alan had creaked along the floorboards until there was no sound apart from the TV and the rumble of Aunty Lorraine's iron. After three hours Uncle Alan crept around the living room door. He cleared his throat and wondered if perhaps I might have seen some of his dice, because if I'd moved them by accident or something then it was best just to say. I said I would go up and have a look, just in case.

Aunty Lorraine wrinkled her lips and watched me as I left the room.

Upstairs the big, bright spotlight hovered over the battlefield, leaving a dark fringe in the corners. Uncle Alan's cavalry had crossed the river and swept around Colin's flanks, hemming in his infantry on both sides and forcing him to retreat into the paper hills. I made a show of probing about in the gloom, pulling the desk drawers out, ruffling the duvet and peering along the window sill. I got on all fours and inched towards the radiator, preparing to feign surprise. I felt a dryness at the back of my throat as I raked my fingers along the skirting board and found nothing. The dice had disappeared.

'Don't worry, Alan, we can finish up without them,' Colin said.

'No, Colin, we can't. Stage five requires attacking armies to be given access to advanced cavalry manoeuvres. We need the dice.'

I wondered if they had rolled along the floor somewhere and laid myself flat under the bed, reaching as far as I could in each direction, but there was nothing. I lay there wondering where they could be, when into the room came a rough panting and the clink of Charlie's collar.

There was a pause, then Uncle Alan's voice filled the room: 'THAT BLOODY DOG!'

A scalding pain erupted in the back of my head as it raked along the wooden slats of the bed and cracked into the side rail. I twisted my upper body round. The spotlight was obscured by an enormous black presence whose grip throttled my ankles, and a glowing fissure of pain seemed to creak along the base of my skull.

'I DON'T KNOW HOW MANY TIMES I'VE TOLD YOU TO KEEP THAT FUCKING DOG OUT!' the shadow boomed.

A short, whining sound came inexplicably out of my mouth as a deep throb began to ring in echoes through my brain. The noise came again, an involuntary nasal whimper I didn't recognise it as a sound I had ever made before.

'Stop it, Ricky.'

I buried my face in the crook of my arm, but still I couldn't stop it. The noise kept coming until it turned into a long, pathetic moan, interrupted by muffled shivers.

'You should have listened to me,' Uncle Alan said, breathing heavily. 'You should have listened.'

But by now I had abandoned myself to a juddering onslaught of tears, and as the throbbing subsided I found myself remembering Sarah's squalid laughter and her sad little table with the chips down the edges.

Eventually I heard Uncle Alan say: 'He wasn't listening to me, Lorraine. I've told him and told him, but he doesn't listen. And now look what's happened.'

*

'Sorry about mess,' Sarah said, dropping ash on the floor. 'Just been sorting out spare room.'

Aunty Lorraine had brought some milk with her this time, although Uncle Alan still made a face at his tea. Sarah said she was all right actually and Uncle Alan said the place looked great, and I wondered, if they couldn't think of anything new, what could I possibly talk about with Sarah after they left?

'We'll come pick you up tomorrow,' Uncle Alan was saying with a crooked smile. 'No rush. I suppose you'll want some time to yourselves.'

I felt an urge to throw myself into the warm, knitted folds of Aunty Lorraine's lap and beg her to take me home, but as she saw me looking she stared in the opposite direction, and I knew I was reading an expression of betrayal.

'He might not even want to leave!' Uncle Alan said, opening his arms and looking around the room cheerfully. 'You've got everything you want here, haven't you, Ricky?'

I nodded.

The black expanse of the window was dotted with distant yellow lights that made the town seem even more remote and obscure than it had before. Soon Aunty Lorraine would be among them.

A difficult silence settled in the room and Uncle Alan shifted in his seat. It was the same look of disappointment as last time, as if he had suggested an excellent game that no one else was interested in. Except this time his forehead glistened, and every now and then he brought a hand up to mop his brow.

'So, Sarah,' he said, 'how have you – '

He lowered his chin as if he were about to belch, and the lank grey hairs around his face fell forward.

' – been getting . . . excuse me . . . how have you – '

His body stiffened, and he brought his fist to his mouth in the manner of someone coughing daintily.

'How have you been getting – '

His head jolted forward and there was the heavy sound of liquid against the floor. Sarah leapt to her feet and let out a little squeal of surprise. Uncle Alan looked up, his tongue hanging out and dripping a thin stream of bile on to the floor. He wiped the lather from his mouth and moved his lips as if to speak, but he simply heaved again, spraying the carpet with lurid flecks of red.

A sour, fermented smell reached my nostrils, and I asked Aunty Lorraine if we should call an ambulance, but she just looked at Uncle Alan. Between convulsions he whinnied as the oxygen squealed along his airways, until the weight of his body tumbled forward, his chin scraping the table as he rolled to the floor.

'I'll call an ambulance,' said Aunty Lorraine, slowly bringing the phone to her ear, and she calmly pushed the bridge of her glasses along her nose.

'Sarah,' she said, once she had given the address, 'what on earth have you had in that cup?'

And Sarah looked at her with an expression of sudden terror, her fingers shaking so that her lighter fell to the floor.

Erica Attwell
The Science of Love

At school, Mr Spears explained to us the science of love. This slight, bespectacled teacher had seen fit to impart to a class of thirty pubescent girls a precious secret. It wasn't the impact on Jennie I remembered – though when I found her in the third-year loos, pants round her ankles, retching and crying for her mum, I do recall wanting to slap her. Jennie should have been grateful not inconsolable; he'd shown us the fundamental atomic basis of every civilised, human interaction: break or be broken. It stayed with me because adults, especially men, seldom tell the truth.

Years later, as I lay on Sam's chest, waiting for the inevitable fall after the rise, tracing my fingers on the buttons of his shirt, I gave thanks to Mr Spears. Without his teaching, I wouldn't know I was one small, stray gesture away from executing the third law. Sam's arm was encircled round me, one hand reaching to the small of my back, just shy of my trousers. His very presence belied his need. If I brushed my thigh to his belt or drew a light finger down his torso, I might set action and reaction in motion and those years of negotiated intimacy would be undone. His mouth might dip to kiss the top of my head and I might turn upwards, and meet those full lips. But I would not.

'Right, hon,' he said, pushing me from him, 'I should be off and leave you to it.' He'd already swung himself round, his feet on the floor, his back bent, hands searching for shoes.

'You don't have to. You can stay, if you want.'

'Stay?' He turned to face me, ruffling his hair with one hand, considering. 'What's happened? You split with Neo-Con Nigel already?' He let out a chuckle. 'Let me guess? Did he refuse to play by the rules?'

Sam reacted like the rest when I tried to teach him, all shaking head and disbelief – as if they could wallpaper the truth with their smiles. They need to wake up, all of them. It's strange: they take for granted the science of economics and evolution, but they don't see that love is the same transaction. Somehow love's molecular level is ignored. People should understand the truth of their singularity, their aloneness. Once they understood that holding was not having, pleasure was just friction, it all made so much more sense than Love or Kindness or God.

'Well,' I weighed the pause. 'Yes, if you must know.' It would be useless to explain, Sam was too prone to believing the danger-ous, civilising romance of courtship, kids and happily-ever-afters. 'Look, it doesn't matter. I just thought it would be easier. No need to make a big thing out of it.'

'Really,' he said leaning back on the bed, his hand propping up his head. He tapped his fingers on the pillow and gave a playful smile: 'But will I be safe?'

'Categorically.' I said, turning my back and pulling off my top and trousers.

'Ha – touché!' he said. 'Don't worry, I know the drill. I'm the good guy you're too scared of hurting, right?' The laugh was hollow, but I noticed he continued to undress all the same. 'Come here,' he said and he switched off the light, dived under the duvet and drew me towards his chest, 'I want your heat; it's cold.'

Once, there had been a possibility – but it had ended as it had begun, clumsily. In the past I've given myself to plenty of men not half as beautiful or generous. But it was too simple. With Sam there was repose and comfort, none of the urgency that needed to be fulfilled. I could never tell him the truth of it, but I thrived on the battle, the harder the better; it made the relenting more enjoyable. It's not contrary – it's science, as my physics teacher said. Mr Spears may not have taught me much – except, now I come to think of it, that force was the product of mass coupled with velocity. But he had taught me that.

We'd been doing an experiment, the one where you put your hands on the glass bulb and your hair stands on end – I liked the effect so much I gelled my hair in spikes for weeks – and we'd all been giggling, like we did, and Mr Spears, he thought we were laughing at the experiment – actually enjoying physics – but we were giggling because we knew Harriet was up next and she had a huge hickey on her neck, courtesy of Alex from the boys' school up the road and, as soon as it was her go, she wouldn't be able to hide it any longer. The glass bulb was passed to Harriet and she played refusenik, of course she did, but Mr Spears – good old Mr Spears – he wouldn't hear of it, he insisted. So there she was, placing her hands on the dome, our eyes on her neck waiting for her hair to rise, voices hushed; he must have sensed something was coming. Then, when he saw it, when the layers of her hair parted and rose in obedience, God, did he blow. Sweet, ineffectual Mr Spears, the only science teacher dumb enough to consider periods a reasonable excuse to skip homework; he lost it. Then, when he'd calmed down, something strange happened: he pushed the desks back against the wall, sat us down in a circle on the floor and explained to us the science of love.

He said everything was made of atoms and when you kiss, when you caress, when you think you are feeling something, you aren't. The reality is you're never touching another human being. What you feel is only the action of atoms banging and jostling against each other. It's funny how many people don't get it. It's as if they missed the physics lesson, were absent that day, because still I see them trying, over and over, to crunch their lives together. Friends, brothers, ex-lovers – it's all the same, they don't see the futility of their effort. They don't see in bringing together the two, they can't ever merge into one; it is never a mutual coming together, but always one person acting on another – forcing, bruising, breaking the other.

'You okay, petal?' Sam whispered, and I could taste his ripe-strawberry richness inches from my mouth. 'I love this moment, just before sleep,' he continued. 'It's so peaceful being here with you,' and he wrestled me closer, tight. I half-wondered if I might snap.

'I can't sleep.' I tried to wriggle free from his grasp, but he held me firm.

'Is it Nigel? I'm sorry about before, I didn't mean to laugh.' He released his hold. 'Do you want to talk about it?'

'No, I'm fine. I'm restless, a bit fidgety is all. Let me shift round a bit.' I shuffled away from him on to my right side, facing the closed bedroom door. 'I'm disturbing you. Ignore me – sleep.' He enveloped me from behind, cupping his body round mine and I listened as his breathing became deeper and more regular.

People fail to understand that Sam and I have a superior understanding, a respected proximity and distance. We'll admit freely to a particular contentment in being in each other's presence – it is unlike any other – but we both respect the line we have drawn. We resist the urge; there's too much at stake. We don't nudge or act on one another; there's no violence or threat in our intimacy. We fit together snugly, like now, the one in the other; two friends who find solace in shared company; it's nothing more.

'Do you want me to give you a back rub, hon, would that help?' His fingers were in my shoulder blades and a delicious, lapping warmth trickled down the length of my spine.

'No, I – ' In truth, I wished he would continue releasing those imagined knots, but reason was victorious. 'We should sleep. But – but thank you, though.'

And yet, sometimes, I do long to long for him. Those hairy thighs, warm against my buttocks; it would be easy to fall back upon him, to bend him to my will, to consume him. I'd gobble him, swallow him whole, he wouldn't stand a chance; it would be a delightful dissolution. But perhaps I'm being unfair, perhaps he might surprise me, and – with the right alignment of the stars – be able to withstand me? I know it's a gentle mania I'm suffering from. I know I can rouse myself from it, but nevertheless I do find myself falling headlong in the hope we might be different; we might transcend the casual encounter of two hazardous bodies. Somehow we might come together, in a mutual coupling and glide, nestled, him and me, captivating the lonesomeness, the one and the other. I could try him now – all it would take is that first act. I might wriggle off my knickers while he sleeps, fling open the duvet, flip over on to my knees and plant myself naked astride him. But there I go again, playing the agitator.

My legs betrayed a tremor. 'Wh – what's up?'

'Nothing,' I said. 'Sorry, I didn't mean to wake you, I just – ' and I rolled over to see him, but in the blackness I couldn't make out his face.

'Want me to put some music on – might help you sleep?' He stood up, a little unsteady on his feet, feeling his way to the stereo in the corner.

I raised myself to look on him and threw off the covers, but he had his back to me. 'Shall I get the light?'

'No, no need,' but he was too slow and the bedside lamp was

on, illuminating me. I flattened my hair, straightened my bra and positioned myself in the centre of the bed before he could turn.

'Well, hopefully this will help.' He looked but didn't regard me. 'Out of the way,' he bounded over. 'Let me back in, it's freezing out here. Oh, that's better,' he said, pulling the duvet over us and rubbing his hands on my forearms and his feet against my shins, 'Good to get a bit of heat up.'

I allowed my body to roll into his and our eyes met. His face was relaxed, drowsy with sleep, but I wondered if those deep-brown eyes understood the mute invitation. If he would just reach down and cup my breast or stroke my thigh, it might begin. I willed him to see the expectation rising up within me, arching up my spine, through my chest and piercing his eyes. If only he would grasp me; the first sally must be his. 'Hang on,' he said and leaned away, 'let me turn the light out.' He rolled over and I was alone, with him on one side of the bed, me on the other. Back-to-back we faced each other in an immoveable stalemate.

I lay there, drifting in and out of wakefulness, waiting with mounting expectation for the offensive. Now was his opportunity; the cover of darkness must give him confidence to strike, now he would make his move. A probing hand might venture forth feeling its way to me and I would meet it. We would be in each other's arms, it might be as I hoped; the stars might be awake in awesome symmetry. Then I blinked and the vision dissolved before me. Everything was still; no hand, no leg, no touch, and I lay there listening to his regular, steady breath. In and out, in and out.

Certainty took over and I felt, very soon, there must be a clash, a grab, something would happen. He would be upon me, his body weighing down, working its way through me and I would have to make a choice: to fight or submit. He rolled on to his back in preparation for the assault, there was a faint murmur and I felt the battle-cry rising up inside me, straining at my chest, burning bitter in my throat. Any second now, it might be, it would be, and I would have to react – he's there on his back now, his hand reaches for mine, there's a low murmur, then there, again, a second time; my heart pumps hard, my chest throbs in the certainty, the loud, insistent certainty that the next murmur, the next movement will signal it's time: he's about to come for me; my lungs are big, full to bursting like an over-stretched balloon. There's no space left, every part of me is taut, at breaking, ready to lift off; there will be a hastening – I will rise up, startled, but he will push down, leaden upon me; then it will be over, as quick as it starts, with a grunt and the crack of his body against mine; a roll, a murmur, bubbling over into a soft, gentle snore – but there was nothing. Nothing came. His murmurs quietened, his breathing slowed, the hand swept back, uninterested, to his warm, soft belly, and I remained untouched and unmoved.

Then I knew the cool, flat reality. There would be no stroke, no signal, there would be nothing. We weren't drawn against or towards each other. I was still playing out that delusion. We termed it respect, but we were like atoms in a vacuum – give us sufficient space and we need never know the other existed. There was me, pitiful and awake on one side of a bed, and him, peaceful and asleep on the other. He had no compulsion to acknowledge me; there was no special irresistibility about me prompting his attention. I was dead to him, unless I acted.

Resolved, I rolled into the centre of the bed, my hand reached over to take him, but just as my fingers made contact, something stopped me. 'This doesn't mean I'm playing by your stupid rules,' I said. But he didn't hear; he was already asleep.

Louise Manson
Angels Fly Economy

'Breathe in, breathe out,' I whisper as I clip my seatbelt into place, trying to distract myself. But this is real. It is really happening. All the weeks of worry and sleepless nights and nightmares are over, I am an actual passenger on an actual plane that is preparing to take off.

For the past two years, I have avoided flying. I don't know why. I have never been in any serious incident involving a plane, nor do I know anyone who was in a plane crash or plane-related accident. It just seemed to hit me one day, two weeks before a holiday in LA, a holiday I had planned a year in advance and had spent most of my savings on. I was at work, standing in the break-out room making coffee for myself, and the realisation dawned on me. The plane could crash and I could die, or I could lose my mind with fear and have to be strapped down and sedated.

I did actually make it to LA and back. But I vowed never to set foot on a plane ever again after that experience. I had survived that flight, but how many more before something went wrong? And if I couldn't cope with a fairly safe, uneventful flight, how would I cope if a real disaster happened to strike? I wouldn't be one of the survivors like in Lost. I would be one of the corpses that the other stronger people would frisk for useful items, then be left to fester shoeless on the beach.

Yet here I am, defying fear, sitting on a plane, ready to go. My counsellor said I should, when I was ready. She told me I should face my fears, not hide from them. To avoid planes was to give in to my fear, and that only gave the fear strength. If I let it, it would consume my life. It had got to the point where, if I saw a plane on TV or in a paper, or even if someone was talking about flying, the fear would begin its crawl up my spine to rest cold on my neck and my throat would begin to close up.

I thought I would ease myself back into this gently, so I'd booked myself on a short flight, Heathrow to Glasgow, LHR to GLA. The flight would be around an hour and my dad would meet me on the other side. I have already texted him about five times since leaving my house, giving him an update every half an hour or so. But now my phone is off and in my handbag. Dad is hundreds of miles away and can't save me. Soon, when the plane is airborne, he will be even further from reach: all the way down on the ground, while I will be miles above the clouds.

'Breathe in. Breathe out. Relax, let it go,' I mutter to myself, trying to remember the relaxation techniques I learned in my counselling sessions. 'It's only an hour. Only an hour. Sixty minutes. Probably only forty-five before they announce descent. You can do this. You are alive and you can do this.'

'Is it too late to get off?' I wonder to myself, as the plane begins to taxi slowly to the runway. Perhaps if I leap to my feet, if I start screaming and fall into the aisle, they will stop the plane and open the cabin door. But I don't. I sit quietly in my seat. I must not think like that. I have created this restriction for myself, only I can break free. The fear is only in my mind, I tell myself. It only becomes worse because I allow myself to focus on the thing, the thing that makes me afraid.

The plane surges with power and moves forward, pushing me back into my seat. All too fast, it gains speed and lurches into the air, leaving solid ground and my stomach behind.

It is now definitely too late to escape. We have taken off. I have to ride it out now. One hour. Sixty minutes. Forty-five minutes until they announce the descent. Probably five minutes until they turn off the seat-belt light. Maybe ten. I can break up the journey, divide it into events, then I will know that time is passing, that it has not stopped, and I am not trapped up in the air, far away from solid ground indefinitely.

The words of my mother from years ago pop into my head. 'Wouldn't you like to be an air hostess, Angela? Just think of all the exotic places you would see?' Yeah, great. I'm sure British Airways or Virgin Atlantic would love to have an air hostess who ran up and down the aisles screaming every time there was a bit of turbulence.

Thinking of my mother brings back more memories. She would begin our visits by telling me how well I looked, which was actually her way of saying I had put on weight. Then she would study my face for a second, to see if anything else was amiss. My hair was looking a bit frizzy perhaps, or my eyelids were puffy, had I been getting enough sleep? Or my foundation was too light, it made me look like a ghost. I remember her constant grumbling, that was how she communicated. She was always a bit dissatisfied with things: the weather, her health, the growth of her herb garden, me. If everything else was fine, she would invariably default to disappointment towards me; she had always wished I had a better job or I was married and had kids by now, and then she would tell me about some schoolfriend of mine I had long since lost touch with who was now having her third child. I think of how frail her hands got as she got ill. It was three years ago, and yet it seems like yesterday that I held her hand as she lay in her bed, in her stained pyjamas which smelled of vomit. I remembered thinking how papery her hands were, and her eyelids, drooping. Then her breathing had become strange. I realise a lump has formed in my throat. I could cry right now.

I allow my eyes to open slightly. I have not moved. We are still airborne. Nothing has happened.

Another wave of turbulence hits and I squeeze my eyes shut again. My stomach lurches and my heart pounds erratically. It is so loud I swear everyone on the plane must be able to hear it. Is it possible for a thirty-four-year-old to have a heart attack? Probably. I take odd comfort from the prospect of dying from that instead of a plane crash.

'You can't stop it, you know,' says a soft female voice to my right. I allow my eyes to open again. Sitting across the aisle from me is a woman I recognise from the frustratingly long queue at the check-in desk earlier. She's perhaps around late fifties to early sixties, and has a thick mop of grey hair and a round rosy-cheeked face with crinkles around her eyes. She is memorable because she was right behind me and I could hear everything she was saying, and while everyone else was suitably irritable about the delay, she was loudly chatting to the couple behind her about how she always tries to think positively and doesn't like to waste energy on negative feelings. I remember hoping that I wouldn't be sitting near her.

'Sorry, what?' I manage.

'The turbulence. You can't stop it. You can close your eyes and clench your teeth, sit really still, hold the armrests really tight as much as you like, but it won't stop the turbulence. I'm Teresa.'

'Angela.'

'Nice to meet you, Angela. I'm also afraid of flying. It's unnatural being so high up in the air in a tube of metal.'

I gulp in some air. 'You seem fine.'

'I've learned to distance myself from fear. It's a negative feeling, fear. Just like anger, or frustration.'

I sigh internally. Was she really going to launch into all this positive thinking stuff again, now? Am I going to be stuck with this for the whole flight?

'Next time you feel like curling up into a ball, do the opposite. Stretch out, relax. Breathe slowly. You can put your seat back and enjoy the flight, and watch the clouds go by.'

'I don't like looking out the windows.'

'You could read, or watch people on the plane, have a conversation like we are now, or even sleep through the whole flight. My point is: do anything you want. You don't control the plane.'

There's a 'bing' sound, and I glance up to see the seatbelt lights are off. Ten minutes must have passed.

'It's not going to fall out of the sky because you stopped concentrating,' she continues. I notice, as she is talking, that her lipstick is a weird orange colour, and some of it is on her teeth. I also notice that her clothes are old, worn-out jeans and a maroon fleece that has gone bobbly, and smells faintly of dog. She definitely looks like a doggy sort of person. 'Are you going on holiday?' she asks.

To Glasgow? Hardly. 'Not really, I'm . . . I'm visiting my dad.'

'How nice. Do you visit him often?'

'I try to. It's been a while since I could bring myself to get on a plane though.'

'Oh, of course. You're so brave. And where's Mum?'

'Mum . . . ' God, this woman knows where to stick the knife in. 'Mum died three years ago.'

'Oh, I'm sorry to hear that,' Teresa says, with genuine feeling in her voice. 'Do you mind me asking . . .?'

'Cancer.'

'Oh, it is a terrible evil, that thing.' Actual tears well up in Teresa's eyes. 'You know, my son also died of cancer, nearly six years ago now. Only thirty-one, bless him. Took him so suddenly.'

'How awful. I'm so sorry.'

'It's an old wound now. But some wounds never quite heal. You never expect to outlive your children. That's something to be feared, more than anything, losing any loved one around you.'

'I thought I was prepared for my mum's passing, but when she actually left me I . . . ' I'm sobbing, I can't help it. Tears are streaming down my face. Other people on the plane are glancing over at me and I feel so foolish.

Teresa stretches her hand across the aisle and rests it on my forearm. 'You're not alone. She's still with you. And she wouldn't want your life to end, just because hers has. It's a really difficult truth to bear, but life does go on.' She rummages in her seat pocket and produces a tissue, which she offers to me. I gratefully accept. Eventually I stop crying. And I feel an odd sense of relief.

'Thank you.' I pat her hand awkwardly with my own. I've never been a tactile person, but somehow this stranger has bridged that distance and, in my desperation, I am allowing her in.

'You know, your mother passing might be the reason you are having these fears. Have you ever thought that?'

'My counsellor said that too. I don't think so, though. Why would my mum dying of cancer have anything to do with being scared of flying?'

'You're afraid of death, dear. And being out of control. You're afraid of flying right now because that is what you are choosing to focus on, but if you allowed yourself to give in to the fear, who knows how far it would go. You might start being afraid of all travel. Then of going outdoors. Then of leaving your house. It's a downward spiral. But it's the control, you see. That's your main problem, allowing yourself to let go, and let someone else be the pilot.'

It's easy for Teresa to be so calm. She's lived her life. I've got so much more of mine to live, so much uncertainty from one day to the next. My nerves scream out for just one day of calm. One day where I am not utterly terrified of everything. One day of boring monotony, when all my achievements are behind me; I've found the perfect partner, settled down, had a child. Even at that thought, I am pained, as I realise my mother will never meet my future offspring. I comfort myself with the thought that I would probably be unable to cope with motherhood and would end up having my children taken off me by social services.

Another wave of turbulence hits the plane. This one is much rougher than the last.

'Now relax. Never mind what your body wants, do the opposite,' says Teresa. 'You want to cower down? Sit up straight. Open your eyes.'

Reluctantly, I open my eyes. The plane is still in the air. I am still sitting in my seat. No one has died. 'Look around at all the other passengers. Look at their faces. Do they look worried?'

I want to be as far away from this annoying woman and this horrible place as possible, back in my nice safe house where nothing can frighten me. I try to focus on her voice, and cast my eyes over the faces of the other passengers. They really don't look fazed. I also find myself weirdly comforted by the notion that the plane is out of my control. Someone else is the pilot, I have no say in what happens. I feel an unfamiliar moment of ease.

'See, you're doing it,' says Teresa. 'And you're keeping an old lady company as well. We can get through this together.' She smiles and squeezes my arm, like we're now best friends.

The plane suddenly jolts again, roughly enough for several of the passengers to gasp. The stewards hurry past with the trolley. I scan their faces as they pass, this time they definitely look a bit perturbed.

Oh my God, this is it. It is really happening. We are all going to die. The plane is going to crash and we are all going to die. I won't see my dad again. I'm going to die all alone in the wreckage of a plane, and my last moments will be spent with this silly old baggage with nothing better to do than to meddle with other people's lives.

I feel the sickening wrench of my gut, a wave of heat pours over me; the old familiar early stages of a panic attack. My throat is dry, like it's stuck together, closing up, I can't breathe. I try long slow breaths through my nose, I try to remember the words of my counsellor, but the memory is on mute, and a million miles away, and all I can feel is red fog filling my mind. It glides across my vision too, so I feel as if I can't see. I clench my fists over and over but there is no release. I feel as if I might explode out of my body with the pressure of this fear inside me.

Then there's a movement on the edge of my vision. At first I can't quite believe what I am seeing. Teresa has fallen forward out of her seat and is in the aisle on her hands and knees. Her face is white, her whole body is shaking, she's gasping for breath. Is she having a heart attack? Oh my God, the poor old dear is having a heart attack right in front of me! I feel guilt and foolishness at being so wrapped up in myself. How had I not noticed that she wasn't well?

I don't know what to do. On autopilot, I unclip my belt hastily and scramble across the seat to her. This scenario isn't on the instructions on the laminated card in the seat pocket.

Other people are staring stupidly but not getting up to help. I try to lift her back up to her feet but she is too heavy. A steward appears beside me, short, with auburn hair and freckled pale skin. Between us, we manage to get her sitting in the aisle, slumped against the side of her seat. He asks me to stay with her, then rushes off and disappears behind the curtained staff area.

Teresa's head looks uncomfortable. I reach for my cardigan from my seat and ball it up to make a pillow. Her hair is flattened on the back of her head; she probably slept like that and didn't even brush it. I kneel down beside her, rubbing her shoulder in a weak attempt at comfort, but I think I am mainly reassuring myself. I keep saying 'It's okay, it's okay.' Over and over, though I know she is not. I feel useless.

Over the aircraft tannoy the steward asks if there is a doctor on board. I didn't know they did that in real life. It occurs to me briefly that I've completely forgotten my panic attack, that I'm kneeling in the aisle, nowhere near the safety of my seatbelt. How long has it been now? I also notice that what I had thought earlier was the plane hurtling towards the earth was in fact just another momentary bout of turbulence, and the plane has now righted itself and is cruising along steadily.

Teresa's face is pale and drawn. She seems barely conscious. I am embarrassed for allowing myself to get into a state earlier. I am a fit and healthy person. Teresa now seems so old and frail.

The steward returns with respiratory apparatus of some kind; a man in plain clothes, who must be the doctor, checks Teresa's blood pressure. He looks concerned. He says something about her heart, then instructs one of the stewards to tell the flight deck that they need medical support on the ground. They try to move her again after a moment, and this time they succeed. Her head lolls and her legs drag like she is a drunk being carried home. They guide her to her seat but leave the apparatus on her face.

Bing. A stewardess announces: 'Ladies and gentlemen, we hope you have had a pleasant flight. We will shortly be preparing for descent, so please put your seats back in the upright position and stow away your tables . . . '

The doctor flashes me a small reassuring smile, and tells me that she should be okay until the plane lands. He probably assumes we are family, and for some reason I don't try to correct him. He and the steward disappear down the aisle of the plane.

Has forty minutes really passed? I can hardly believe it. I realise I feel fine. Absolutely fine. In all the commotion of trying to help Teresa, I have completely forgotten my fear.

We begin the descent. More turbulence rumbles through the cabin. I feel that silly fear, like a petulant child sitting on my shoulder, whispering absurd things, when in reality there is no need to be afraid. I feel myself distancing myself from it, and thinking of other far more important things, like getting Teresa to an ambulance. Of stepping off the plane on to solid ground. Of seeing Dad's look of relief when he catches sight of me in the terminal.

I watch houses and fields and streets below rush by. It dawns on me that we could still easily die now. The plane could still flip, land upside down on the runway or, worse, on top of a row of houses. The wheels could fail, and we could crash into the airport buildings, or land nose first and explode on impact. I imagine all the worst things, but I sit upright in my seat, my body is relaxed, and my eyes are open. I hold on to Teresa's hand and accept oblivion, for now at least.

Rick Bland
Before It's Too Late

Mom, I don't want a Catholic funeral! I scream it as loudly as I can but as usual my parents don't listen to me. At least they have an excuse this time. Supposedly I'm in a coma. They whisper. They cry. I listen, hungry to find out what happened. I was having a biopsy to see if the tumour next to my heart was cancerous and now my parents are in Dublin deciding whether or not to turn off my life support. Fuck.

After years of doubting my parents' love, their sobbing astonishes me, ebbing and flowing as they take their time to decide my fate. I am their baby, their only girl. From what I can tell, my arms are folded, resting just below my chest, above the stiff, starched hospital blankets that cover me. I now live via sound and smell . . . A buzzing smell of bleach fails to hide a swampy marriage of bed pans, soap, body odour and abused food. I worry when my stomach starts to crave the food . . . the intravenous line fills me with nutrients but my stomach rages at its emptiness. But I adapt. I have no choice. The percussive sound of shoe soles now defines time, distinguishing bustling mornings from expectant visiting hours and from the eerie quiet of the night. Every waking moment I attempt to move my fingers or open my eyes, to signal I'm in the room. After five days of nothing, my body has become my coffin.

I wanted my parents to know I was happy. Finally. After years of hard work, I was finally getting the hang of life . . . then I visited that doctor . . . and he made his stupid diagnosis . . . Six months earlier I opened my Pilates Studio and its success is wowing. And just after I arrived in Dublin, I met Conor . . . when I told my parents 'I'm dying for you to meet him,' I hadn't meant it so literally.

I should turn thirty in two months. On 24 January 1993, I moved from Toronto where I'd felt as if an invisible hand had taped a plastic bag around my neck and forced me to run a marathon. When I told Mom I was moving to Dublin, she said, 'You're just running away.' I argued 'I'm running to . . . something.' It was breath . . . Until now, Dublin made me dizzy, as if overdosing on oxygen.

In Toronto, I had been more likely to find a unicorn or a dodo than love. Sure, I fell hard a few times, but love was always one-way. Was I ugly, deficient, or simply unlovable? Lust was just as rare. If a hot-blooded Torontonian had to choose between sex with a chaste nun, a hole in the wall or me, I'd always be the bronze medallist. Add a leper to the mix and I'd be pushed off the podium. It got so bad, I considered going out for Halloween as a 'fuck me' sign. My friends thought I was joking . . . so I pretended I was.

At the end of my first week in Dublin, I take myself out to Temple Bar for a Guinness. The bartender takes four minutes to pour my pint. Every second I wait is a pleasure that is trumped by my first sip. Heaven is silky brown. I raise a glass to my new life and my thoughts slip out a bit too loud: 'To me,' I say. That's when I notice Conor gazing from across the pub. I laugh. Then stop. He must think I'm insane. I immediately look over my shoulder to see what he's staring at – all I see is an empty chair. He approaches. I move out of his way so he can sit, but he keeps smiling at me. My dreaded blushing begins, all my blood migrating rapidly to my cheeks. I drop my head. Move further out of his way. His big feet, in beige North Face trekking boots, remain planted in front of me. I look up. Apologise. He smiles. Confused, I ask, 'Do I have ketchup on my face?' He laughs, so I explain, 'I just ate a rather large hamburger.' He counters, 'I don't believe it. Where did you put it? I mean, you're utterly . . . ' The pause hangs in the air. I want to ask, 'Utterly what?' He exhales, smiling, eyes locked on me. My cheeks bubble with blood. He asks, 'What's your name?' His blue eyes, contrasting with his curly black hair and white skin . . . wow. And he asks again and I'm blushing so much I can't speak.

I excuse myself. Run to the washroom. My vision narrows but I navigate my way to safety. Safety? Conor is blindingly beautiful and I run away. Idiot. No wonder I'm single. It's not too late . . . I'm going to find him and buy him a drink. I pull myself together. I leave the washroom as Jim Morrison sings and I practically crash into Conor, who is waiting with a freshly poured pint of Guinness. 'Fuck,' I say.

'Well, for now, a thank you will do,' Conor says. A laugh flies out of my mouth as I say, 'It's just I was hoping to buy you a drink.'

'You can get the next one. If I don't bore you to death.'

'Well . . . ' I take a deep breath. I look up. As if he could bore me. His bass voice vibrates inside of me, tickling. I smile and say,

'I hear Guinness tastes better in Ireland.'

'Everything tastes better here.'

'Everything? Really?'

And he nods 'yes' slowly and says, 'Do I detect a Canadian accent?'

'Good guess.'

'I spent two summers working at a restaurant in Toronto called Spinnakers.'

'At Queen Quay?' I ask and he says, 'You know it?'

I continue, 'I love their fish and chips, especially the tartare sauce. I could eat it with a spoon – maybe you served me?'

'No,' he says.

'You sound certain.'

'I am,' he says conclusively, his smile so large it threatens to connect at the back of his head, 'I would never have forgotten you.'

I feel chemicals going off in my body – how are my clothes staying on?

Come On Baby Light My Fire reaches its finale and he leans in. He smells of Eternity and a hint of garlic, 'So what is your name?'

I almost ask, 'Are you blind?' but instead I just say, 'Hi, I'm Eileen.'

*

I've been in hospital for a week. Life's memories liquefy. I flow in and out of them.

I'm five. I see a million possible futures but I'm boiling with fever. No one is sure if I will survive. A hooded figure sits in a chair, long thin fingers flipping through my favourite book, *Matilda*. One possible future is highlighted. It's short, coming to a full stop because of a six-foot-deep hole. Will the figure take my hand and lead me to it?

I'm older. To cope with the disease of high hope, my mother has learned to suffocate dreams like a farmer drowns a bag of kittens. One dinner, my favourite dream floats out of my mouth, 'I'm going to be a dancer.' Mom pounces, saying, 'No.' Dad gets up and leaves silently.

'Why?' I ask.

Mom starts to clear the table even though I'm still eating. Taking my plate, she says, 'You're just copying Jane.'

Jane is my cousin.

'I don't copy her.'

And Mom rolls her eyes.

'I have a mind of my own.'

'Then use it.'

'I'm trying to.'

'Just because you want something doesn't mean you'll get it.'

'Shouldn't I try?'

As she leaves with a stack of plates she says, 'Be a nun. God will stay true to you . . . unlike . . . ' And she stops, staring ahead, plates shaking. Mom runs to the kitchen, takes her pills, her shaking subsides and she starts cleaning our spotless house. I learn that every mention of dance hurts her. So I bury that dream. Dance becomes my secret shame. I'm not good enough, not pretty or leggy or interesting. Mostly, I'm not Jane.

One day as Mom weeps, I say, 'Mom, I will be a nun.' Her tears stop. A smile fixes on her face. A rare moment I make her happy. So I commit to being a nun . . . and my reward is sweets . . . weight starts to appear on my boyish frame.

Time passes. Jane is nine months older but years wiser. We're both twelve. I'm tempted to ask Mom if she'd prefer to have Jane as a daughter, but I'm too afraid of the answer. Then Jane is accepted into the National Ballet School of Canada, four hours away in Toronto. I remember Mom saying, 'She'll be running the place soon.'

Though I keep saying I will be a nun, I'm lying. I don't want to be a none. A nobody. I'm already exceptionally good at that. But it gives Mom joy. And I'm a dutiful daughter. I consider treating her as she treats me . . . I perfect what I'd say . . . 'Mom, there's something tragic about a semi-retired secretary, spending her nights watching TV with her husband, reading romance novels passed down to her by her dead mother.' I choose never to say it.

When we're thirteen, Jane comes home for her summer break. My weight gain is noticeable. Jane says nothing. One day I ask, 'Can I tell you my secret?' 'Yes,' says Jane. I um and ah and um, then finally let it out, 'I want to be a dancer.' Jane smiles. I drop my head.

Deep humiliation flushes my cheeks: how could I, a fat, disgusting nothing dare believe . . . I want to snatch my words back and eat them . . . it's all I'm good at . . . Jane interrupts, 'You should dance. Expressing yourself through movement is the best kind of freedom.'

I understand Jane. I know that she sees me.

That summer, Jane teaches me ballet in her room every day. The first lesson she says, 'Eileen, you have perfect dancer's feet and amazing turn out,' and I burst out crying. Her compliment changes something in me.

Summer flies by as if it's been released from a cage. At its end, Jane returns to Toronto. I want her to stay. I'm overtaken by dread. It feels as if nothing will ever be the same again. But I'm selfish. Jane shares dance with me and yet I want to hold her back. As I hug Jane, she makes me swear to continue dancing, her parting promise; 'At Christmas, we will do two classes a day.' And we hug. I won't let go. She pries me off her. I wave until the car is out of sight.

Jane doesn't keep her promise. A truck carrying sand tips on her car just outside Toronto. Jane and my aunt are gone in an instant.

When I emerge from my grief, I'm a two-hundred-pound blimp. One night I swallow forty of Mom's anti-depressants. The hooded figure returns. We have a staring competition and I wake up, projectile vomiting all over my bed. I'm too fat for death to bother with . . .

Or has death given me another chance?

For once I grab it and secretly enrol in a dance class. I tell no one. I'm filled with equal parts of joy and shame. When I want to quit, Jane's memory pushes me through it. And every class hurts so much. I HATE the way I look. The studio is full of mirrors. When I catch sight of myself, moving left, switching direction, my skeleton moving right . . . my bulk keeps going left for a short time, before switching direction, so I avoid the mirror. Time passes and I transition from hiding, red-faced, at the back of the pre-beginner class, to leading the professional class. I emerge from my fat, like an Eskimo carving emerges from soapstone . . . The Eskimos claim the sculptures have always lived within the stone . . . the artist just reveals what is already there.

But even if you take the fat away, the fat girl remains . . . Mom makes that clear when she finds my tights drying in the basement.

'What is the story behind these?'

And I tell her I'm studying dance.

'Really?'

'I have been for three years.'

'That explains the change.'

'For the better, I hope.'

Mom pauses and looks at me with contempt before continuing, 'You aren't Jane.'

'No. I'm alive.'

'For now . . . '

'What does that mean?'

'Don't you want to be a nun?'

'No. I never wanted that.'

'Never?'

'Never!'

She absorbs this like a body blow.

'If you really want to dance, why hide it?'

'Because I knew you'd react like this.'

'You think you know so much?'

'Mom, I'm actually really good.'

She doesn't believe me. But the next day I get my first job. And as my career soars, my personal life flatlines. Mom appears a supportive, proud mother. She sees all my shows. But she never says anything to me. Ever. Absolutely nothing.

*

During the biopsy, something went wrong. My heart filled with blood. I didn't breathe for eight minutes. I died. And was revived. Officially, I'm brain-dead.

I don't know if I'll ever find out why it happened. I do know a decision has been made. Mom, Dad and Conor are about to say their goodbyes. I keep trying to signal I'm in the room . . . but life is slipping through my immobile fingers.

My parents ask Conor if he'd like to be alone. He cries. My mother hugs him. Time passes before he says, 'I'm okay.'

I'm so envious of her. Mom and Conor part.

As my parents' footsteps recede, Conor nears. I smell him mixed with Eternity. My desire hurts like a third-degree burn.

'Okay, your parents are gone . . . it's safe to wake up.'

He kisses me. His lips are warm and soft. He continues,

'I'm serious. Wake up.' And there's a pause. 'I know you're in there.'

I listen to him breathe. He's confused.

'Fuck . . . you really are gone!' He pauses then, 'When I first saw you . . . I had this image . . . the two of us holding hands and running into the future, screaming YESSSS!'

Just then two children run past my room, laughing. I lose contact with Conor. Where is he? Has he left, leaving his beautiful smell hanging in the air like a ghost? The answer falls on my lips in the form of a tear. His salty sadness touches my tongue. Eventually, he continues . . .

'I want more of you. I'm greedy. I miss you. Your absence has swallowed me. I was sure we'd grow old together. So wrinkly that our faces would fall to the ground like accordions . . . and we would have to help each other pin them back before beginning yet another day. Come on, my bubbalicious. Please.' And as I lie there, I scream a silent yes. The silence stretches and I hear sadness spasm out of him. He manages to say, 'Goodbye . . . lovely.' His words ooze love, exquisitely beautiful and bruising.

I feel that I've been seen fully. Completely.

My parents race in to comfort him. Conor apologises. My dad says, 'Son, never apologise for loving Eileen . . . ' and Dad stops himself . . . he can't talk about me . . . he will connect to the deep well of sadness that lives within him . . . so he forces it into a space shared with all his other regrets . . . compressed like carbon, diamond hard. It's my parents' turn to say goodbye.

Dad's is simple. 'You are my . . . greatest joy.' He chokes up. I smell Old Spice then hear my parents touch. I feel their love. Over the years it has expanded and contracted as violently as their current grief. Mom takes my hand, 'I've never told you this, Eileen. I dreamt of being a dancer . . . but my mom put paid to that. Yet I behaved just like her. You made me so proud, the number of times I almost burst. I'm ashamed I never told you this when I had the chance . . . I did want you to thrive . . . more than you'll ever know. You were such a gentle, innocent, beautiful soul . . . I couldn't bear to see life hurt you . . . I'm so sorry . . . '

I want to tell her we did our best. That life isn't what happens to us. What really reveals who we are is how we handle what happens to us. I don't want her to think of me and feel bad but I'm powerless. Mom will have to figure that out herself. Or not. Then I understand . . . somehow Mom's instincts told her that dance would lead to this. Suddenly, her overbearing cruelty and coldness flip and become overwhelming love.

I work madly to move my fingers or open my eyes. I want to let them know that their goodbyes showed me I was better than I ever imagined. If only I'd lived knowing it. Then the doctor enters. Fuck.

'Is it time?' asks my mother. 'Yes,' says the doctor. She lets out a moan saturated with sadness. My lifeline is unplugged.

The hooded figure enters the room. My heartbeat begins to

slow. My life becomes a pool of memories. The memories are my story . . . it is vast . . . it is tiny. It is mine. Life begins to close in around me. Grief pours out of my mother and floods the room. Dad takes her to his chest . . . her sobbing muffled . . . he finally exhales . . . I swear I feel my finger move. Conor sees it . . . asks the doctor. 'It's involuntary,' he says to Conor. The darkness encloses . . . the beep of my heart slows. A tear pours down my cheek. Conor says, 'She's crying.' The machines slows. The doctor says, 'That's unusual.' Is that enough of a sign? I try to scream, 'Turn on the machine.' I count my heartbeats . . . one . . . two . . . three . . . Mom is far away, speaking . . . four . . . saying something about a Catholic funeral . . . five . . .

A. C. Macklin
Corpus

Wexler Square was huge. Mercy had never seen so many people in one place, and they were all staring at her. She remembered Brother Tourville in front of the Synod and lifted her chin. She wasn't going to be outdone by him. Pride might be a stupid thing to hang on to at such a moment, but it was better than nothing. Better than giving them all the satisfaction of watching her beg.

The escort cleared a path through the crowd to the raised platform at the centre. A Brother stood next to a stake piled high with brushwood. She stumbled up the steps as the chains snagged, but the collar-pole held her upright. She was forced in front of the Brother. He narrowed his eyes.

'Mercy Danann,' he said, in a voice pitched to carry. 'You have been found guilty of blasphemy. Recant now and your spirit may yet be saved. Do you recant?'

She looked past him at the crowd. Humans, elves, goblins, all watching hungrily. They wanted her to burn. Sheep, the lot of them, so terrified of uncertainty, preferring to kill than think something new. None the less, they were her people. She had to warn them.

'The gods are waking!' she shouted. 'Run! Run before they kill you!'

The crowd roared their anger, drowning out further words. The escort sergeant glanced at the Brother, who nodded. Three men leaned on the collar-pole, pushing her forwards. Three more waited with ropes to bind her at the centre of the bonfire. She resisted, leg muscles tensing. Her feet slid out of control.

The pole pushed her inexorably nearer. The platform gave way to brushwood. She screamed, bringing all her strength to bear. It wasn't enough. Her head was forced against the stake, mashing her nose. Ropes bit cruelly into her skin. Her breath came in shuddering, angry gasps. There was no give in her bonds, no hope of escape, but she kept trying.

The noise of the crowd was deafening. A sound beyond words, the baying of a pack that's scented blood, surging around the platform. When the torch was brought out a note of frenzy entered the howling. They wanted to see the flames eat her. She screamed back, hating them. Hating Grandfather, who brought her to this. Hating Astraeus, for not being the god she'd thought.

I don't want to die!

The Brother brought the torch into her field of vision. With ceremonial slowness, he lowered it to the brushwood. For a moment nothing seemed to happen. Then it caught in a leap of yellow. A haze shimmered as the fire took hold, scrabbling fingers of flame spreading up and round. The crowd retreated into the background. Her awareness narrowed to crackling and smoke and the first lick of heat against her calves. A scream became uncontrollable coughing. Tears streamed down her cheeks.

I believe in the gods of air, I believe in the Stray God, they won't save me, I don't want to die, oh gods I don't want to die . . .

Her vision darkened. Smoke swirled up in a corkscrew. Burning filled her lungs. Tight pain spread through her legs, till she could think of nothing else.

A voice came out of the sky, rolling round Wexler Square like thunder in a barrel.

'KNEEL.'

She wasn't screaming any more, she realised. It was other people, the other side of the fire. Every scale on her body prickled. A blast of cold air hit from above, punching away the smoke and guttering the flames. Dust and rubbish were flung up into the crowd. More screams. Then he was there, hanging in mid-air over her head, blazing with light and utterly impossible.

'Astraeus?' she whispered. She felt numb. He was alive. He was alive, and here for her.

He spoke again, louder and more terrible. 'RELEASE HER!'

The sound rode the wind, which had embers in its tail; bright sparks caught on banners and clothing. Tongues of fire licked up around the square. People in the crowd began to panic, the beginnings of a stampede. Astraeus raised one arm and the smoke poured up to form a swirling ball around his fist. The other pointed accusingly at the Brother, who was staring slack-mouthed.

'Release her,' the Stray God said softly, 'or all the pains of my recent years on you will be repaid.'

The Brother didn't move, his face ashen with shock, but the nearest guardsman drew his bayonet. He clambered up to Mercy and hacked through the ropes, cutting her several times, though she felt nothing. When the last few strands parted she held out her chained wrists. He unlocked those as well. They scrambled down to the platform together and the guardsman fell to his elbows in abject begging. Astraeus descended, reaching out to her.

'Come to me.'

She took a wobbly step. Then, absurdly, the Brother reached for her shoulder. Astraeus's face creased with anger as he drew himself up. Mercy dived for the ground, arms over her head, as a pillar of smoke blew down and enveloped the man. She heard a ragged scream, quickly cut off, and the roaring of furious winds. The

crowd was in full flight now. She crawled to the edge of the platform and slid into the chaos.

Which way should she run? It was impossible. The current of
panicking bodies swept her away from the platform. People fled
towards the Temple for sanctuary, instinctively turning towards its
solid walls and leadership. They poured through the doors and into
the nave like a rip tide, finally slowing into little scared eddies.

Mercy found herself pushed up against a column, stuck between
a fat elf who stank of tobacco and a couple of human boys. She
could see out of the main doors to where, having finished with the
unfortunate Brother, Astraeus blazed into the sky.

'MERCY! COME TO ME!'

White light flared and he vanished upwards. She could still hear
people screaming outside, their cries punctuated by the rattle of
muskets as the Guard arrived at a run. A line formed across the
Temple door. Mercy looked around for an alternative escape route.

The nave stretched hundreds of yards to her right. Spiralling
pillars held up a beautiful mosaic ceiling. Benevolent cloud-faces
peered down from the roof, punctuated by golden lanterns on long
chains. Tall windows of plain glass ran the length of the building,
revealing drab houses on one side and lush private gardens on the
other. At the far end, behind the purple-clothed altar where the
statue of the Stray God ought to be, rose a pair of massive square
doors. They looked ancient, the wood black with age and the metal
cross-braces completely rusted. The lanterns nearest the doors
swung slightly, their flames leaning away from a constant draught.

*Those must be the Gates of Paradise, which means the home of the gods is just
the other side. Well, where else would Astraeus go?*

She worked her way slowly through the crowd, using her
elbows and hips to shove people aside. It took a good ten minutes,
by which time they were already starting to forget their terror.
Some even had the emotional capacity to complain about a goblin

pushing past. She ignored them, concentrating on her goal. She could feel the icy breath fluttering under the gates as she neared. The crowd was much thinner here. No one wanted to stand too close. She went right up to the wood and gave an experimental push. The gates didn't move at all – they didn't look as if they ever would again. She put her shoulder against the enduring structure and heaved.

Nothing.

'Oi!' A skinny woman carrying a basket of holy icons stared at her. 'You're her. The heretic.'

'No.' Mercy gave the gates another shove.

'You are. I got a good view. You're her. Oi, guardsmen! Over here!'

'Shut up!' Mercy gave her a furious glare.

The woman backed away and kept shouting. Other people started to look, mouths opening like fish. A bow wave built up as the Guard pushed through the crowd.

Mercy hissed in frustration, thumping a fist on the wood. The place she had to get to was just the other side, but there was no way out here. She looked around wildly. Then she saw an entrance to a small stairway, tucked away behind a pillar. She ducked under the lintel and took the narrow steps two at a time. They spiralled tightly up, slippery from use. There was a latched door at the top. She opened it a crack, as quietly as she could.

An empty vestry lay behind it, lined with dark cupboards for the Brothers' vestments. She couldn't see any other doors. A dead end. Going back wasn't an option, not with the watchful crowd and the approaching Guard. At least here she could limit their approach. She'd have company when they took her down. Better a rat in a trap than roasted.

An old cabinet stood just inside the door. She opened it. The sight of crystal decanters made her realise how thirsty she was. All that screaming and smoke had taken its toll on her throat. She shut the door and hauled the cabinet in front of it. Then she picked up the decanter labelled 'wine' and took a deep, grateful gulp. It was far better quality than she was used to, filling the back of her nose with a raspberry fragrance. She choked slightly and drank again. The pain of swallowing began to ease and the trembling in her arms slowed.

One of the cupboards slammed open behind her – a hidden door to the outside world. She spun, hurling the decanter. It smashed against the lintel in a shower of crystal shards and wine. The figure in the doorway ducked, one arm over his head.

'Fuck!'

'Vigor?'

He shook himself, dislodging bits of debris. A slice across his ear began to drip blood on to his collar. 'You stopped for a drink? Come on!'

She followed him out at a run. They skidded right into a long corridor. A cry went up behind them, then the sound of urgent pursuit. They pelted along the carpet. Vigor tugged her sideways through an archway on to a wide balcony. It jutted away from the building, stopping just inside the swirls of endless mist. Mercy stared.

'This is the place you told me about.'

'No time for sightseeing,' Vigor said, glancing back over his shoulder. 'Get ready to jump.'

'Jump?'

'No other way out.'

'But – '

He dragged her towards the balustrade. 'It's only one floor up. Roll when you land, you'll be fine.'

She wanted to give him a hug but there wasn't time. She climbed over the stone rail and looked down into the shifting grey.

'I hope you're still looking out for me, Astraeus.'

She heard a loud yell behind her as the Guard arrived. 'Stop her!'

'Jump!' Vigor shouted.

She let go, and dropped down into the realm of the gods.

Petra Einwiller

The Other Side

Sabine had set out with Edward at lunchtime. The morning had been promising, and though rain clouds had eventually begun to hover, there was still space for the September sun to shed its flattering light on the town.

They were in Edward's car on Fleet Street, slowly heading towards the City. The midday traffic was thinning out. He was wearing blue jeans and a fine-knit black cashmere sweater and she wondered whether she was a little overdressed in her rose-embroidered organza skirt.

Sabine leaned against the window to let the sun warm her face. She hadn't been able to shake off the odd feeling all morning. A couple of days ago, there had been that old Hispanic woman talking to Edward, who'd mysteriously stalked off when Sabine had approached them. Then, last evening, that middle-aged man in the gallery. Thinking about it, there'd always been someone who wanted to talk to him. What did people want from him? Was she reading too much into things, or was Edward hiding something?

'You're quiet,' he said.

They were passing the Daily Express building. Sabine looked around. 'I love the art deco design, the black façade, the round corners.'

'The ceiling in the foyer is covered by a single silver piece shaped like a leaf,' he said, 'With a pendant lamp illuminating it.' He smiled at her. 'Never seen anything like it.'

They crossed Blackfriars Road and St Paul's Cathedral came in view.

'Are you taking me to St Paul's, then?'

'If I told you, it wouldn't be a surprise.'

She bit her lip and crossed the fingers of her right hand under the seat. The last time she'd been there had been almost thirty years ago. She'd tried to climb the dome and panicked.

It all came back. She was a ten-year-old on a school trip, brown uniform, ponytail, going up on the cold stone steps, trembling all over, a frightened little creature. She recalled the feverish cries of her classmates ahead of her, the people she didn't know pushing past her, and the piercing voice of Miss Haverston behind her. 'Here you go, step by step, just imagine what awaits you up there. London at your feet! Isn't it exciting?' No, it wasn't exciting, she didn't want London at her feet, she wanted to go home and crawl into bed with a book. 'Go on, we don't want the others to wait.' If only Miss Haverston would shut up. She was really trying. When Sabine slowed down even more, Miss Haverston's irritated voice pressed her on. 'It's not that difficult, Sabine.' An icy brush of wind came through a small opening in the wall. It felt like a whip in her face, and she started crying. She turned round to Miss Haverston and wanted to say, 'I'm scared,' but then she saw the cold disappointment in her face.

Edward drove round the cathedral, heading north. He had to stop at a red traffic light.

'Sabine?' He put his hand on hers. 'What's the matter? Talk to me.'

She looked at him, at his light green translucent eyes. His unhurried moves and calm voice were soothing, as if nothing could get to him, but at the same time he saw through you. Being with him felt like being in his orbit. Talk to me. Edward never acted disengaged, didn't change the subject or pretend not to notice when things got uncomfortable. He couldn't be more present. Was that what drew people to him?

But what about the man in the gallery last night?

That incident long ago at St Paul's had taught her one thing. Pretending everything was fine when it wasn't never worked. Putting off her questions would only make things worse.

Edward stroked her cheek. His touch was tender. 'You want to ask me something?' he said.

The traffic light changed to green.

'You did it again,' Sabine said. 'You know what I'm about to say before I say it. It's kind of creepy. Like yesterday in the gallery when you talked to – '

'Carl.' Edward took the first on the right into Gresham Street.

'You were both standing close to me. I couldn't help overhearing the conversation. Charlotte introduced you to Carl, so he clearly didn't know you . . . ' She studied Edward's face. His expression was blank. 'But after just a couple of minutes, he told you he was afraid he'd lose his business.'

'Perhaps he was embarrassed about not buying.'

She shifted her body in his direction. 'Then you told him someone he'd trusted had talked him into a bad deal where he'd lost a lot of money. That's odd.'

His eyes were fixed on the road. 'It's what usually happens.'

'I mean you telling him.'

No answer.

'Do you know the person who did this to Carl?'

'No.'

'Did someone tell you about it before you two met last night?'

'Look,' he said. There was stress in his voice. 'I was trying to help.'

'Carl didn't seem to think so, he was quite upset.'

Edward parked the car in front of a large office building fenced by a metre-high wall. They were not far from St Paul's, a five-minute walk away. They got out of the car. Sabine stepped in to a sunken garden with an old fountain in its middle. It made a perfect refuge. Some City workers sat on benches quietly eating their lunch.

He came up beside her. 'There was a church here once. It's the original font.'

'It's beautiful,' she said.

He pointed to a free bench. 'Shall we sit down?'

For a moment they sat in silence, amid the smells of earth and jasmine. Sabine was entranced by the garden, it had a Zen-like feel. She turned to him. 'You have an understanding of people that's almost as if you can read their minds. I thought it was just mine, but it's other people too, isn't it?'

Edward sat very still.

'You know things about people you shouldn't know. Are you involved in something dodgy? Because if you really wanted to help Carl . . . ' She shook her head. 'What you told him, how did that help?'

'If I was up to something, why would I tell Carl what I knew and make him suspicious? The truth can hurt. He had to understand.'

'What business is it of yours, what happened?'

'I helped him see what he couldn't see.'

'But how could you know?'

A woman in a blue suit on the next bench was staring at them. When Sabine looked back at her, the woman packed her lunch wrappers in a paper bag and left.

Edward got up. 'It's getting late.' He left the garden and she followed him. That wasn't how it should have gone. He was supposed to have explained things, set things right.

She caught up with him. The clouds had thickened, a gust of wind made her close her jacket. They crossed the road and turned into a small lane, heading towards St Paul's.

'I'm worried about you. About us,' she said.

He glanced at her and took a deep breath. 'I can see when something's wrong. Call it a sixth sense.'

'You saw in Carl's face that someone tricked him.'

His voice was level. 'No, I had to go into his mind, and see what's there.'

She stopped, facing him. 'You messed with his head?'

'It's not what you think. I only saw what Carl wanted me to see. And it doesn't happen with everybody, I need to feel a connection. Besides, with you it's different.'

They'd reached the end of the lane. Across the road St Paul's was resting majestically, like a lion after a feast. Damn. She let out a little groan.

'What happened there?' he said.

She moved away from him. 'What?'

'I told you, I feel I know you. If you really know someone, you don't need words. What am I thinking?'

'Please don't.'

He took her hand. 'The first thing that comes into your mind.'

At his touch, Sabine softened. She could try. She shut out all thoughts and concentrated on the feel of his touch. It was crazy, but something came. 'You're sad that I refuse to see what is between us.'

He squeezed her hand. 'That's right.'

'You could just be saying that.'

'I would never lie to you.'

She remembered the moment their eyes had met. Was it really only a few weeks ago? At first she'd been startled, but then she saw the surprise and amusement in his eyes, as if he was glad to see her after a very long time, as if there had never been a question of them meeting. And then she felt a sense of familiarity, as if she'd deciphered a coded message, and she was glad to see him too.

'I don't want to be meddled with,' she said.

'I would never harm you or anyone,' he said.

She looked away, then back to him. Perhaps he was right, perhaps it wasn't so hard to read someone's mind if you watched out for the right signals.

Two minutes later they walked up the two flights of stairs to St Paul's main entrance, through a revolving door on the left-hand side, and were immediately confronted by the ticket office.

'Sixteen pounds fifty?' Sabine said, turning to Edward. 'I don't want to pay that much!'

'You don't have to.' He paid for them both.

'I'm afraid the Whispering Gallery is closed to the public today, but the viewing platforms are open as usual.'

She moved away from Edward, further inside, and was astonished. St Paul's wasn't the dark, reverence-demanding place of her childhood memory. The size of it! She had to bend her head all the way back to see the ceiling; the large clear windows let in a lot of light; the marble walls and statues were creamy-white; there were candles everywhere. She felt a wonderful sense of openness and space and light. They didn't have to go up the dome. They could just wander around here.

Edward came up behind her. 'We're entering the danger zone.'

Sabine shot around, alert. 'What do you mean?'

'My father believed religion makes people weak, enslaves us, stops us from seeing what's real.'

She looked at him for a moment, then started to walk down the right-hand isle. 'I was brought up a Catholic by my mother. She wasn't devout, but cared enough to send me to church every Sunday until I was ten, after first communion. Then she relaxed.

'In church it was always dark and cold and damp. I imagined this was how it must be in a tomb. And then the priest telling you about your sins, punishment and salvation. Now, here,' she smiled, 'I feel at peace. Perhaps I believe I'm forgiven.' She looked up at the painted ceiling. 'I still wish I could touch it.'

'The divine,' she heard Edward say.

Their eyes met. She stepped closer to him and touched the wooden pendant around his neck. Its geometrical surface was perfectly crafted and felt even and smooth. The simplicity of it was beautiful.

She said, 'Some people say when we're born, we have parts of our former selves in us, that the past stays with us, that we never forget who we were.'

'Do you believe that?' he asked.

'I don't know. Sometimes I come to a place I've never been and I think I've been there before, but can't say why. I meet someone I've never met and feel I know them. It's scary.'

'Why?'

'Because if it's true, we have no control. We're haunted by the past.'

'We're all haunted by something. But we have to face our demons.'

'You want to make people remember bad things.'

'Yes.'

'Why?'

'I don't exactly make them. They come to me. They want help. Deep down they feel something's there and doesn't go away. All I do is make it tangible. We have to go through pain – '

'Excuse us,' an elderly American couple pressed past them. Sabine realised that they were at the bottom of the stairs leading up to the dome. She felt a flutter in her stomach and her mouth went dry.

'What's wrong? Are you afraid of heights?'

'Yes. No. It's not the height. It's . . . ' she hesitated. 'It's a high open space.'

She felt Edward's gaze on her. Then he said, 'It's the drop.'

She looked up the flight of stairs, ascending into darkness.

'If you don't want to go, it's okay. But it could help you.'

'I'm not sure.'

'If you make it to the top, you'd be rid of your fear.'

'Perhaps another time.'

'It's your choice. I don't want you to do anything you're not sure of.'

Something so simple, like going up some silly stairs. This wasn't like last time. He wasn't like Miss Haverston, he gave her a choice. She took the first step, and the next. Edward was behind her. There were so many people. Their voices echoed back from the stone surface. She had to brace herself, tell herself to breathe steadily. The stairs were worn, slippery. *I can do it.* Her head started to spin, going round and round in circles. The echoes in her head became louder, she heard children's voices, laughing, panting.

'Excuse me,' a girl said, hurrying by, forcing Sabine against the cold wall.

'How much further to go?'

'We're halfway there,' Edward said.

They passed the big bell and continued going up. Her legs took one step after another but they didn't feel like her legs, they were somehow disconnected from her.

'Centuries of secrets are buried underneath these stones,' Edward said. He was right behind her, but his voice was like a faint signal, coming from a place far away.

They reached a platform high up within the dome, a metal grid with tiny gaps in it. She must not look down. Another flight of steps. A hand was on her sleeve, Edward was saying something, but she didn't understand. His mouth moved, but his voice was muffled as if it was behind thick glass. He shook her gently and she came back round. 'You don't have to do this,' she heard him say.

It was too late. She needed air, she needed space, badly. She held tightly on to the metal railing, made herself gaze up and put her foot on the first step.

'She's so slow,' a girl said.

'Shhh.' A woman's voice sounded like a snake.

She moved upwards. She felt the cold air before her eyes saw the light, the exit. She felt her way forward, slowly, trembling, on to the viewing platform. Beneath her feet the stone was grey and hard. She was so cold. She was still holding on to the rail, she couldn't let go. Her feet touched the edge. The ground looked peaceful from up here, she could just let go.

'You did it!' Edward's voice drew her back. 'Just give it a minute, you'll be okay.'

Then the panic came. She was shivering with fear, she wanted to cry, but not in front of him. 'Leave me alone!'

She rushed back into the darkness, frantic, and hurried down the stairs, pushing people aside. Finally she was out, in the open.

Edward caught up with her. 'Sabine!'

'Why did you make me do it?'

'I thought it would help you. And I was right. You made it to the top, then all of a sudden you panicked. God,' his eyes were wide. 'You're dead pale.'

'You call this help? I don't need this.'

'Next time it will be easier.'

'There won't be a next time. I know what's wrong with you. You get inside people's heads, you make them do things they don't want.'

D. H. Yeats
Bugger! Bugger! Bugger!

The bell is sounded. Left, right, left, right. For an instant the old soldier is confused and thinks it's parade time. Left, right, left, right.

She takes his hand in hers and softly presses it. Her touch is warm. It makes him feel safe. Now she leans over and kisses him on the forehead. 'Goodbye, my darling,' she says, a look of concern and sadness on her ravaged, once pretty face. Then she turns away from him.

He watches her walk along the centre of the ward towards the exit.

Left, left, left my wife and twenty-four children without any gingerbread. Do you think I did right, right, right?

Her sensible-heeled shoes clicking on the surface of the scrubbed and scoured lino floor as they propel her past phlegmy coughs, blood-curdling cries, imploring yells, grunts of frustration and despair from ignored supplicants.

By Jove I did a good job for my country when I left, left, left!

But it is she who's leaving, not him. How he wishes she could stay. He tries to shout out, to call her back, to plead with her to remain longer. But the words just won't come; he feels them way down in his throat, they are quite stuck. He who was once a weaver with words can only emit a splutter. A sense of abandonment surges through him.

He tries to sit up, hoping she will turn around one last time before she exits the ward, hoping to be noticed, but strength evades him. It is only after she has gone through the door that one word quite suddenly erupts from deep down in his throat. 'Bugger!' he howls. 'Bugger! Bugger!'

The male nurse, who was all smiles when his wife arrived two hours earlier, scowls. He has seen this nurse metamorphose many times into the embodiment of sadism. He watches that flabby frame as it lumbers over towards his bed, chin and cheeks swathed by a five o'clock shadow that appears blue in the ward's dim light. He notes the clammy pallor of the skin, the unhealthy fleshiness and those thick glass lenses which give the eyes a beady, bird-of-prey look. He would never pass muster, wouldn't hack it in the army that's for sure, he thinks, the old soldier again as his voice rises to a crescendo:

'Bugger! Bugger! Bugger!'

The nurse's puffy blue face is swooping down over his. He can see his own reflection in the moonlike glasses. He suddenly recalls the story of Bluebeard. Where was Bluebeard's castle? Wherever was it? Where? He tries to remember.

'That's enough from you.' The nurse speaks quietly, so no one else can hear. 'Or it'll be the lift for you. Mark my words.'

In Pornic it was. Now I remember.

Fortunately the nurse's anger is diverted by the entrance of the supper trolley. He finds himself unceremoniously hauled up to a seated position, a table placed over the bed, trapping him further. Then a plate containing some strange-looking gruel is plonked down.

This place is nothing like that hall they sent him to when he was wounded in 1917. He met her at that hall. His wife. Where is she? Wasn't she just here? Name? Name? Oh sweet Jesus, what is her name? It's not that bloody woman, not Mother. What on earth is it?

A tear forms in his left eye.

And that hall to where he was sent, whereabouts was that? Some or other noble lord's pile turned into a hospital. In Cheshire? She was a nurse there, more like angel. A hospital staffed by angels. We were treated with respect there. Like heroes. She had pushed him in a bath chair through the grounds. It must have been autumn. Michaelmas daisies, yes there was an abundance of Michaelmas daisies which became their favourite flowers. Yes, it must have been autumn.

There is only one orderly flitting from bed to bed to spoon-feed him and over twenty others and, with no one else to help him, his own lame attempts ensure that most of his supper finds its way down his front on to his bed.

A quarter of an hour later the beady-eyed one is prowling along the ward droning, 'She loves you, yeah yeah yeah,' something he seems to do with an irritating regularity. That woman, yes his wife – oh, what is her name? – told him laughingly that they were lyrics from some current popular song.

The beady-eyed one comes to a halt at the bottom of his bed and emits an exaggerated sigh. He looks up. It's Bluebeard again. Bluebeard's castle? Where was it? Oh yes, it was in Pornic. It was calm in Pornic. The calm before the . . . no, not a storm, he thinks, it was much worse than a storm.

'What a nuisance, you messy pup, can't you do better than that?' the nurse says.

It was like being on holiday in Pornic, then. In that tiny little Breton fishing port with golden sandy coves, cider served in ceramic bowls and pretty girls on bicycles. Where was that postcard he brought back? He must find it. Where did he put it? That old hand-painted postcard of the harbour and the castle. He showed it to his grandson once. You must go there one day, Sonny Jim, he told the boy. Yes, how he would scare all his grandchildren with tales of Bluebeard. You see that castle in Pornic once belonged to him. That's right. It was Bluebeard's castle. Why is there so much evil in the world?

'I suppose we'll just have to clean you up again, won't we?'

Did I survive the trenches in the First War for this? When he was a small child his mother, at the kitchen sink, would roughly wash him behind his ears and around his neck, getting rid of the grime. But that was his mum, she cared for him. What they do in this place is like torture, like punishment.

'Come on! Try and sit up!'

Those trenches were riddled with disease. He feels a strong pang in his belly, remembers with terrifying clarity those dirty, smelly trenches, the bodies waiting to be buried out in that mudbath they called No Man's Land.

They take the bodies out from here in the night time. He's seen them. They do.

'Ouch!'

Where did that sound come from? Did he make that noise? Was it from within or without his body?

'I didn't hurt you. Stop wriggling. If you can't sit up by yourself, I have to lift you up.' The beady-eyed one scrubs his face with a coarse flannel. It feels like an army of ants are crawling over it.

Life in those trenches was so monotonous. It was futile to fight the vast army of rats or the plague of frogs found in waterlogged shell-holes. Fighting the Hun was futile, too. We only had to do it again twenty years later.

'Right, that's you sorted. Now I don't want any more trouble from you tonight.'

He is strangely calm yet silently perplexed as he rides the waves of memories. How did he come to be here? He was useful once when he believed that he was striving against injustice, fighting for freedom, fighting the war to end all wars. He was feted as a hero. But now is he a baby again? He feels a twinge in his left shin. He had a wound there. A serious leg wound led him to her. Out of tragedy came . . . oh ruddy hell, what's her name?

Hell's bells and buckets of blood! The beady-eyed one is coming this way, the orderly one step behind. Take cover. Left, right, left, right. Left my wife . . . her name? What's her . . . phew, close one, all clear! They've gone past.

He drifts again, war and wounds are left behind and he is young, not yet tainted by those conflicts to come. He is striding in the golden July sun along the footpath beside a field of ripening oats, behind his family home. A dog is running beside him, a book of verse is under his arm, he can see his destination: the shade of an ancient oak. He would spend hours seated there with his back leaning up against the trunk, solitary, reading, while he lost himself in another world, whose beauty the real world could only fail to emulate.

The lights go out. He needs to piss. He attempts to sit up, fails desperately. He tries to call out for help. He is going to burst. Flood gates will soon open, dams busted. He is in an absolute frenzy for the indignity of that bottle. Now two more words float up to the surface, and like a stuck gramophone record he starts to repeat:

'Come on! Come on! Come on!'

The beady-eyed one starts to slowly lumber down the ward.

Left, right, left, right.

'Come on! Come on! Come on!'

But by the time the beady-eyed one reaches his bed with the bottle, draws back the sheet, pulls down his pyjama bottoms and tries to place his penis in the bottle, it is too late. The flow has already started and cannot be stemmed. They couldn't stem the flow of the sea into that ship which sunk either. What was it called? No, better not utter its name.

'Come on! Come on! Come on!'

'Enough of your come on, look what you've done now. What a nuisance you are!' The nurse's hand rises as if he is about to lash out but there is a cough from the orderly and instead he lets the penis drop. Once his pride, it lies sore, red and shrivelled.

'Not much to write home about there, and now we have to clean you up. Yet again.'

But it is the orderly who is told to do it.

When the orderly has finished, and he is wrapped up in crisp white sheets, his mind drifts back to Pornic. Where is that postcard? How he'd like to see that postcard. He felt safe in Pornic. It was in Pornic, in June 1940, that they'd heard a ship was coming. He'd been travelling the length of France seeking a boat on which to escape back home. And then, suddenly, there was one coming in to a nearby port. What was its name? Oh, that's it. St Nazaire. St Nazaire, yes. He'd erased that name from his mind many years before. No, mustn't talk about it. It was an official secret. He'll be court-martialled if he lets the cat out of the bag.

He opens his eyes. The beady-eyed one is staring down at him.

'There's nothing for it. We'll just have to open the window behind you now. We've got to get the smell out of here somehow.'

Of course the enemy knew. It was the British public that were kept in the dark. But he saw it all. There were over five thousand embarked already. Then suddenly the bombers were circling, the Junkers swooping down for the kill, strange metal birds not imagined back in 1914. It only took twenty minutes for the Lancastria to sink. The old girl just rolled over. The sea was on fire. He was frozen to the spot. He watched in horror until he could no longer. Nearly two thousand never officially accounted for, just written off as casualties of the land war. Keep mum or you'll be court-marshalled. Disgraced. Finished.

He hears that now familiar sound of the sliding open of a sash window behind him and immediately feels a blast of the icy air around his head. Now the light behind his bed is switched off and the beady-eyed one and his assistant dissolve out of his sight.

A second could be a minute, a minute an hour and although he had been sleepy, now he cannot sleep. The cold air gets beneath the covers and he is unable to cuddle up, to pull the blankets over his head to keep out the cold.

He knows cold. He grew up in cold houses, waking up to delicately-patterned ice crystals on the windows, but this cold which takes hold of him starts to bring back memories of the flooded, frozen trenches, how his eyebrows and the hairs in his nostrils stiffened. Back then his whole body was constantly numb with cold, continually shivering for days on end, while his mind was tormented by a nagging feeling of apprehension, of fear beyond fear. But he had his rum ration to raise his spirits then. How he could do with a tot now.

I will go to sleep, he orders himself, I will. But still he lies wide awake until he just cannot abide it any longer. That word has come again to his mind, teasing him, coaxing him on. He feels it forming in his throat, rising. He tries to sit up but his arms can only flail like those of a rag doll. But that word is now surging up, an under-water explosion rising from within his depths.

'Bugger! Bugger! Bugger!'

How long this staccato, machine-gun noise lasts he cannot say but it's remarkably soothing, its repetition a balm to his condition, rhythmically lulling him towards a more pleasant place. He becomes aware of whisperings around him, but doesn't care.

'Bugger! Bugger! Bugger!'

He hears the beady-eyed one call the orderly.

Left, right, left, right.

Bluebeard's fleshy face is hanging above his.

'Right, that's it! I've had enough of this. You know the score.'

'Bugger! Bugger! Bugger!'

The orderly is standing at the bottom of the bed and starts to pull at its frame and he is swiftly transported out into the centre of the ward.

Now, panting, the beady-eyed one is shoving from behind.

Left, right, left, right.

The bed clangs and groans as it is propelled the length of Nightingale ward. Grunts, whimpers and coughs assail him from either side, but still he continues to yell:

'Bugger! Bugger! Bugger!'

'I'll give you bugger, you stupid old fool. I should have gone home by now. You've made me late,' the nurse hisses. 'You know where we're putting you. You'll have time to think of effing bugger in there.'

The bed is roughly pushed through the pair of swinging doors at the entrance of the ward, jolting him. They manoeuvre him out into the draughty corridor. He has been through this routine many times before and he smiles as he realises he will soon be left in peace.

'Get the door, Jim,' the nurse orders.

Now he hears a different sound, of scraping, concertinaed metal.

'Bugger! Bugger! Bugger!' He yells as if his words can actually propel the bed onward. 'Bugger! Bugger! Bugger!' His voice rises to a crescendo, approaching jubilation as he looks up and sees the familiar low ceiling of the lift above him.

Once the bed is securely in the lift, the nurse and the orderly retreat and the door slides shut. He hears their fading voices as they make their way back towards the ward.

'I'll be off now, Jim. Just time for a swift one in the Castle,' the beady-eyed one is saying.

So Bluebeard's going back to his castle. Where was that castle? Pornic, yes!

'I'll be back in the morning. Goodnight. I expect the rest of the night staff will be here soon.'

''Night.'

He can be silent now. He is alone. No more gut-wrenching stenches to endure, no startled cries in the night and no icy draught. He starts to warm up, to feel as if he is sheathed in cotton wool.

The bars of his bed dissolve. The sides of the lift appear to disintegrate.

Shrouded now in bright sunlight, he rubs his eyes and draws back his bedcovers. A delicious tingle runs up and down his spine as he sits up in the bed and then swings his legs over its side.

He is actually standing. He is upright again after so many years. He looks around him and finds himself at the bottom of the path behind his house. He can hear children's laughter. A dog is barking. It's his dog. He has it on a lead. It's pulling him. He lets it lead him to her. She says his name and reaches out her hand to him. He says hers. It's Grace. Yes, Grace.

Now they are walking in those fields. Once they reach that old oak, they lie down beneath it and he starts to read her a verse from the book he takes out from the side pocket of his jacket:

> And David's lips are lockt; but in divine
> High-piping Pehlevi, with 'Wine! Wine! Wine!
> Red Wine!' the Nightingale cries to the Rose
> That sallow cheek of hers t' incarnadine.

Her soft angel hair cascades over his chest. Beside a wide-brimmed straw hat, a tiny baby is contentedly gurgling as the sweet squeals of delight from three young children, playing hide and seek, echo across the nearby cornfield.

The golden sunlight becomes more intense. It gradually transmutes into a white light; so very bright yet not at all blinding. For a single moment he sees everything around him with a tremendous clarity.

*

At six in the morning the orderly is whistling as he goes to open the lift door. He's looking forward to going home and his bed. The beady-eyed one is just lumbering by on his way back into the ward. The orderly cries out.

'Effing hell!'

'Language, Jim! What's the matter?'

'I think he's dead,' the orderly replies. His face is white with shock and he is shaking.

'Well, you'd better wheel him back in the ward, clean him up and then in ten minutes you can go and fetch the doctor on call. Whoever that is today.'

Debbie Ash-Clarke
from Fusion

The leather-bound chair outside the Dean's office was lumpy and hard. What on earth did he want to see her about? Sophie felt sweat gathering under her armpits.

The door to the Dean's study opened and Katharine Stott appeared in the slit. What the hell was she doing here?

'You can come in now, Sophie.'

Sophie rose and entered the room, which was wood-panelled and furnished in rich, dark fabrics that looked as worn as the Dean and his pinstriped suit. He sat behind a huge wooden desk while Katharine perched on a chair off to the side.

'Come in, Ms Kingsbury, come in. Sit down.'

The Dean had wispy grey hair and a goatee beard. His cheeks were papery white against his red, swollen nose. He'd always seemed remote from the students, even from the postgrads, and Sophie had barely spoken to him before.

'Ms Kingsbury, you're a postgraduate student in Theoretical Physics, supervised by Professor Romain. Is that so?'

'Yes, sir.'

'Are you aware that it is against the rules of the University for students and staff to engage in sexual relationships?'

Oh God. 'Yes, sir.'

The Dean cleared his throat. 'And how would you characterise your relationship with Thomas Romain?'

'We work very well together.' Sophie grappled for the best words to use.

'And is your relationship purely that of student and supervisor, or would you say that there is a personal dimension to your relationship?'

Sophie hesitated. She didn't like liars, but neither did she want to get Thomas into trouble or get herself removed from Keble.

'We socialise together sometimes,' she parried.

'And are you having a sexual relationship with Professor Romain, Ms Kingsbury?'

Sophie's eyes dropped to her lap. She hated liars. She hated liars!

'Yes, we are. But it's only been once or twice, just recently, and we realise it's not right. We will stop.' Sophie heard words coming out of her mouth as if someone else was speaking them.

'That hasn't been my impression,' Katharine interjected. 'On the contrary, I think it's been going on for months, hasn't it, Sophie?'

'Is this true, Ms Kingsbury?'

Sophie missed a beat. 'Yes.'

'I'm afraid to say, Ms Kingsbury, that this is a most unacceptable state of affairs. Most unacceptable. I'm sorry to tell you that Professor Romain can no longer be your supervisor.'

Sophie stared at the Dean. 'What do you mean?'

'We will have to assign you a new supervisor. It may not be at Keble but it will be somebody from one of the Oxford colleges.'

'But my PhD is in Thomas's specialist field. I'm not sure how it would work with someone else whose field doesn't cover . . .'

'Ms Kingsbury, there is no point in discussing this. I will be speaking to Professor Romain and he will be asked to explain his conduct, but I will tell you something: you will not be continuing to work with him. It is most inappropriate. If we cannot match you with another professor at Oxford then you are free to make your own arrangements elsewhere. Is that clear?'

Sophie felt her throat constrict. 'I've nearly finished, sir. I'm in the final stages of my thesis and . . .'

'Ms Kingsbury, it is out of my hands. This is the University's policy.' The Dean had been looking at her as they spoke, but now he averted his eyes. He looked irritated, wanting to move on to the next thing. 'We will contact you about making alternative arrangements for your PhD supervision. In the meantime, I suggest you do not fraternise with Professor Romain on college premises. That is all.'

Sophie's mouth fell open and she rose from her chair, glancing at Katharine as she turned to leave the room. Katharine gazed at her with open schadenfreude.

'Can I appeal against this?' Sophie said, turning back to address the Dean.

'Are you aware,' Katharine said suddenly, 'that Thomas is a married man, Sophie?'

'He's not. He's not married, Katharine.'

'I'm very much afraid, Sophie, that he is. And if he has never told you that, then that tells you everything you need to know about Thomas Romain.'

'That is all, Ms Kingsbury. You may go,' said the Dean.

Sophie left the room in a daze. She made her way to the toilets where she ran cold water over her wrists and wiped her eyes. After regaining a modicum of composure, she made her way to Thomas's office, where she knocked and pushed her way in without waiting for his reply. Seated inside were four undergrads, arranged in a semi-circle around his desk.

'Sorry,' she said, ducking out of the room again, her face burning.

Thomas came to the door and stood in the opening. 'What's

wrong, Soph? I'll be done in about . . . ' He checked his watch. 'Five minutes or so. Wanna come back then?'

Sophie nodded and walked quickly away down the corridor, into the kitchenette. On automatic pilot she filled the kettle and flicked it on, but she didn't make a drink. She pulled out her phone and texted Carina: 'In the shit. Just been told Thomas can't supervise me any more xxx.'

Less than a minute later Carina texted back: 'Omigod, Soph. What r u going to do? xxx.'

'Gonna speak to Thomas. Will then come home. Spk later xxx.'

Sophie left the kitchenette and went back to Thomas's office. This time she stood outside and listened to see if the students had gone. She heard a babble of voices and then the door was yanked open and three of them came out. One of them lingered, talking to Thomas about something. A lanky girl with long dark hair. Pretty.

Sophie barged in and flung herself on to the sofa. Thomas finished his conversation with the student and she left the room, glancing at Sophie.

'Sophie, I've got a lecture in fifteen minutes. What's up?'

'So the Dean hasn't spoken to you yet?'

'No. What?'

'He's suspended my PhD.'

Thomas looked astonished. 'What?'

''Cause we've been seeing each other.'

'How the hell does he know that?'

'Katharine. Who else?'

'Fuck.' Thomas came over and sat down heavily on the sofa beside Sophie. He seemed lost for words.

'And Katharine said some shit about you being married . . . '

'Oh, did she?' Thomas scowled.

'It's . . . it's not true, is it?'

'Of course not.' Thomas seemed uneasy. He got up and started pacing around the room. 'So what's going to happen about your PhD?'

'They will assign another supervisor from Oxford, and if I'm not happy I can go find one elsewhere.'

A deep groove appeared in Thomas's forehead. 'I'm so sorry, Sophie. This shouldn't have happened.'

Sophie slumped against the arm of the sofa and closed her eyes. She felt drained. But Thomas seemed really agitated.

'Tell you what, Sophie. Let's go for a drive.'

'A drive. Where? I thought you had lectures?'

'Only one. I'll ask John to take it. He won't mind – he owes me a favour.' Thomas strode from the room leaving Sophie on the sofa, her mind doing somersaults.

When Thomas reappeared a few minutes later he picked up his jacket and checked he had his wallet with him. 'Let's go, shall we?'

'Where?'

'Come on. Where's your sense of adventure?'

Down in the car park, Sophie slid into the front passenger seat of Thomas's Citroen. It was a nice car, much smarter than Sophie's little Fiesta. Thomas pulled out of the car park towards the A34, then turned south towards Newbury.

'Where are we going? To my mum's?'

'No. I just want to . . . Let's just drive, Sophie.'

Sophie looked at Thomas's face in profile: his straight nose and strong jaw, and those sparkling brown eyes which were always so full of mischief. He was concentrating on driving but there was something else in his expression too.

'I need to tell you something,' Sophie said, as they passed the turn-off to Abingdon. 'But not while you're driving.' She could see the speedometer from her seat: they were travelling at ninety.

'What?'

'I'll tell you when we stop.'

'Tell me now. I can talk and drive. Parisian men can multi-task.'

Sophie considered whether now was the right time. She needed to tell him soon.

'Oh, just spit it out, Soph.'

'My period is late.'

'Your . . . what?' The car juddered slightly as Thomas glanced towards her.

'My period. I haven't had one for six weeks. And this morning I did a pregnancy test. I'm pregnant, Thomas . . . '

'Sophie, Sophie, Sophie, Sophie. *Putain de merde!* Is it mine?' The speedometer crept up, almost a hundred now. Thomas put his foot down and whizzed past a car travelling around seventy in the inside lane.

'Of course it bloody well is. What kind of a question is that?'

'Just checking. I thought you might have got bored with this old body of mine.'

'Hardly.' Sophie's voice was a whisper, her throat dry.

'What are you going to do?'

'Isn't it something for us to decide together?' Sophie couldn't take her eyes off the speedometer and wished now that she hadn't brought it up while they were in the car.

Thomas didn't answer. They approached the junction with the M4 and he left the A34 to join the M4 heading for Wales.

'Why don't you tell me where we're going?'

'Just a place I like. I'm glad you brought up the . . . new problem. We can decide on it all in one go. Us, this . . . your career.'

'You can't even say it, can you? Pregnancy. A baby. This is your child I'm carrying.'

Thomas flicked on the radio and turned it up. Radio Four. *Gardeners' Question Time.* Thomas didn't give a shit about gardening but Sophie knew what he was doing: blanking this. He didn't want to talk. She leaned her head against the head restraint and let her eyes close.

She should ring Granddad. She should have gone to see him. Everything had been so . . . full-on the last couple of days. 'Wherever we're going, can you drop me in Newbury on the way back? I need to see my mum and Granddad.'

'If you like.' Thomas sounded sulky.

The sky was blue with patches of white cloud, and brightened as they neared the Severn Bridge. Over the bridge, past Newport, through Cardiff, then Thomas indicated and left the motorway at J34, turning south towards Cowbridge. The roads became smaller and they were driving through farmland. Even the A roads were small and wiggly. The sea came into view on the horizon: blue-grey and choppy, laced with white horses. Thomas pulled into Nash Point car park, a gravelled area near the cliff, and stopped the car. There were only two other cars there, and no one to be seen.

'Fancy a walk? I've got a coat in the boot if you want.'

Sophie got out. It was chilly on the clifftop in the breeze, but the view was gorgeous. Thomas went to the boot and got out a navy quilted coat which he passed to her. She slipped it on.

'What about you? Will you be cold?'

'I'm never cold,' he said, folding his arms in front of him.

Sophie shrugged. The wind was bracing and cut through her jeans, making her flesh throb. She followed him towards the edge of the cliff, hanging back as he peered over the escarpment.

'Look,' he said, reaching back for her hand, encouraging her forwards. Something fluttered in her chest but she let him pull her towards the drop. The edge was almost sheer, the rock grey and flaked, the dark sea churning below. As a climber she had no fear of heights, but a respect for them. And since her friend Josh had died she hadn't wanted to take risks.

'What do you think?' he asked. 'Do you like it?'

Sophie stumbled on a stone under her feet and pulled back from the edge, breaking contact with Thomas's hand. 'Yeah, it's nice.' She brushed her hair away from her face. 'How do you know it?'

'Oh, I come here sometimes. It's a special place. When I need to think I like to drive around.'

'I meant how did you find it?'

Thomas shook his head. Then he pulled Sophie to him and they stood together in the weak, late afternoon sun, the cold air biting into them, staring out to sea, watching the clouds chase each other. Sophie could feel Thomas's arms around her wiry torso, could feel why she had never doubted she wanted him in her bed.

'What Katharine said about me being married . . . ' he said.

'It's not true.' Sophie replied.

'No, it isn't. I was telling the truth about that. But I have lied to you about something else. Lied by omission.'

'What?' Sophie turned to him, his arms still around her.

'I'm sorry.' Thomas dropped his gaze. 'Marie and I . . . when I said that we were no longer together . . . '

Sophie pulled away. 'You and Marie, you're still . . . '

'Yes. I'm sorry.' Thomas looked away, staring at the horizon. 'I am so sorry, Sophie. I've been a shit.'

'Six months, six months we've been seeing each other and you never thought to mention . . . '

'When it first happened I thought it would be once or twice, that you'd get bored of me, want a boy your own age. I never thought . . . '

'So you lied, all this time? I can't believe it, Thomas. I can't.' Sophie moved away from him. She wanted distance between them. All those phone calls with Marie: he'd said they were all about Thierry, their son, but no. All the time he was still with her. And that explained why he so often went back to see them, too.

Sophie turned and hit out at Thomas, but he grabbed her arms and held them. 'This won't help,' he said.

Tears came to Sophie's eyes. 'I can't believe it. You lying shit.' All the fight had gone out of her.

'Sophie, Sophie, I'm so sorry.' Thomas pulled her against him. 'I could leave her now. Is that what you want?'

'I don't know what I want!'

'What about . . . the pregnancy? What do you want to do about that? Will you . . . get rid of it?'

Sophie flinched. 'I don't know.'

'Do you even want kids?'

'Yes. One day. For sure.'

'But you're, what, twenty-three?'

'Twenty-four.'

'In the middle of your PhD . . . '

'Not any more, am I? And that's your fault too.' Sophie knew she was being unfair. Their relationship had been entirely consensual.

'Sophie, Sophie, Sophie . . . I love you.' Thomas blurted. He'd never said it before.

Sophie stared at him. 'Do you?'

'Yes. Yes, I actually think I do.'

'What a fucking mess,' Sophie said. She turned and walked back towards the car, her head bowed. Thomas followed her.

'I love you, Sophie. Wait . . . I'll leave Marie. We can be together. You can finish your PhD somewhere else, with another supervisor.'

He grabbed her shoulder and swung her around to him, then took her face in his hands and kissed her.

She felt weak with desire.

She put up no resistance as he pushed her into the back seat of the car.

Author biographies

Debbie Ash-Clarke loves both words and fiction. She has worked as a magazine sub-editor and writer. The extract in this anthology is from her first novel, *Fusion*. Her story, 'No Longer Home', appeared in the *Stories for Homes* anthology. Her second novel is a thriller about animal rights. Debbie blogs about writing, flexitarianism and weight control.

Erica Attwell completed the basic and intermediate creative writing courses at the CCWC between 2011 and 2013. Since then, she has written the first draft of her novel, *The Taxonomist*, and is starting a PhD in creative writing at Goldsmiths, University of London. Find her on Twitter @ericaattwell.

Lizzy Barber was born in 1986 and lives in Islington, north London. She read English Literature at the University of Cambridge and is currently a marketing manager. She is the author of *Cabana: The Cookbook*. 'Café' is part of a longer work, inspired by the life of her grandmother.

Kate Beswick grew up in Hollywood, has a BA from Smith College and an MA (distinction) from Middlesex University, where she won the short story prize. She won the Litchfield-Time Warner prize for her first novel, *Stay in The Room*. She has spent most of her career as an actress, on Broadway and at the Royal National Theatre and the West End. She is a fluent Russian speaker and her Russian background was the inspiration for her most recent novel, *Year of Night*.

Rick Bland worked for twenty years as an actor in the West End, on tour and developing new work. His critically acclaimed, award-winning play *Thick* was performed on both sides of the Atlantic. He is developing his latest play *Full of Bees* at the Park Theatre and writing a series of short stories. He writes, acts and works as a freelance animation producer.

Natalia Bulgakova has a degree in philology and psychology from Moscow State University and worked as a freelance journalist and diplomat with the Russian Foreign Office before moving to the UK to continue her studies at the University of Cambridge. She lives in London, dividing her time between working for a British think-tank and studying early twenty-first-century Russian history.

Petra Einwiller was a criminal lawyer and then worked as a journalist. She has a particular interest in exploring unusual connections in unlikely places. She lives in London. 'The Other Side' is part of a supernatural thriller set in contemporary London where a woman falls for a man who can see past lives.

Lee Farnsworth has a PhD in molecular biology. He spent more than fifteen years working with pharmaceuticals and medical devices, including a spell as European business head for one of the world's best known pharma brands. He now divides his time between consultancy and writing. 'Woman's Hour' is taken from his first novel, *The Birdman of Acton*.

Ben Gareh lives in London with his wife, two children and their ageing Boston terrier. He has been writing mainly short stories for around five years and is currently working on a coming-of-age novel set in Istanbul and London. This is his first proper publication and is a stand-alone piece.

B. B. Howe has found her creative voice after a period of profound loss and writes of betrayal, endings and new beginnings. Drawing on her personal experiences of moving from one continent to another and back, the legal profession, motherhood, early widowhood and being a sole provider, B. B. Howe writes of raw emotions and twists of fate. 'The Peaches' is an extract from her first novel.

Mark Hudson is a writer and former journalist and a trustee of an NGO which mentors ex-offenders. His short story in this collection comes from a novel-in-progress called *Beyond the Black Gate*, a story of abuse, love and early Christianity, set during the collapse of the west Roman Empire in the year 409.

Rachel Knightley is a writer, director and teacher of creative writing, speech and drama. She won the 'Promis' Prize (London Writers) for her short story 'The Existence of Tim' and has written for stage and radio. Rachel lives and teaches in London while completing her first novel, *Anything but Summertime*, for a PhD at the University of Hull.

Lucinda Labes is a London-based journalist. A graduate of the Creative Writing MA at the University of East Anglia, Lucinda is completing a novel based on the Paris diaries of her ancestor, Gouverneur Morris. Morris wrote every day as the Revolution exploded around him. His love affair with the married Comtesse de Flahaut forms the heart of the story.

A. C. Macklin writes fantasy novels and short stories. She lives and works in London, while studying for an MA in Creative Writing at Middlesex University. This piece is an extract from her second novel, *Corpus*, which follows Mercy as she tries to get revenge for her father's murder and accidentally causes a religious revolution.

Louise Manson was born in 1985 and grew up in the north-west Highlands of Scotland. She has been an aspiring writer from a young age, drawing inspiration from her surroundings and the people she meets. She now lives in Hertfordshire with her wife and dog and, when not writing, spends her time painting landscapes and seascapes.

Stuart McLean was born in Warrington and currently lives in St Albans, working as a laboratory manager. A keen reader and writer of crime fiction, he was shortlisted for the inaugural CWA Margery Allingham short story competition. 'Mad Dog' is an excerpt from a recently completed novel.

Jay Norbury attended the Complete Creative Writing Course intermediate and advanced courses in 2014. He lives in the north of England.

Sarah Park wrote her first short story at the age of seven in a blue notebook, bringing characters to life in scrawly handwriting. The notebook has long gone but the bad handwriting remains, as does her love of storytelling. She works in PR, is a qualified journalist, and lives and writes in London.

Carina Swantee is a Swedish/Swiss national who has lived in London for four years, where she has studied English, art and photography. She has followed courses in creative writing at Richmond Adult Community College and at the CCWC. 'Sunsets Over the Bay' is an extract from her work in progress.

Kate Weinberg studied English Literature at the University of Oxford and did a Masters in Creative Writing at the University of East Anglia. She spent most of her twenties and thirties not